The Emerald Necklace

I0592483

ANNIE SEATON

The Heirloom Search:
Book 1

The Emerald Necklace

First published as:

Capturing the Pirate's Heart

Copyright © November 2014, Annie Seaton.

ISBN 9780648399049

DEDICATION

My lifelong love of history has been enriched by reading historical fiction over the years. Authors like Mary Stewart, Sharon Penman Anya Seton and Diana Gabaldon are some of the wonderful authors who have fed and nurtured my love of other historical periods and must be acknowledged as key influences in my writing journey.

To all of the historical authors I have read and loved over many years, this book is dedicated to you.

Prologue

New Orleans 1794

Josephine du Bois closed the door quietly and stepped into the inner courtyard of the mansion on Rue Toulouse in New Orleans. As the violet sky of dusk deepened into full darkness, the chirping of the cicadas was replaced by the croaking of frogs in the cypress swamp across the garden. The sounds were familiar to her; she would spend many hours in the cemetery which divided the street from the swamp. She waited, her head tilted to the side. The wind lulled and the sounds of the night stopped suddenly, as if the conductor orchestrating the chorus of nature had lowered his baton.

She would be patient. The night had eyes.

Despite the garden being in the centre of the sprawling timber building, she must be certain no one was watching when she buried the parcel she clutched tightly to her chest. But fear still gripped her in its cold hands. No matter if the owl perched low in the branches of the magnolia tree spreading across the opening above her head, stared at her with hollow eyes, or the frogs swimming in the ponds on the side of the courtyard sensed her presence. There were no houses to the east as the great conflagration of 1788 had destroyed the stately homes of her neighbours so no human eyes could watch her from high windows as she completed her task.

Josephine limped across to the circular brick garden and caught her breath as the arthritic pain gripped her hip like a vice. When Francois had claimed this land for them in 1769 and built their home, the Spanish style of an inner courtyard had appealed. It had been in the early days of their marriage when all was well.

Despite the pain, she smiled. Francois had been trying to keep in favour with the Spanish governor until the cowardly official had fled back to Spain the following year, but the inner garden had served her well in the many years since then. Now the heady fragrance of the late flowering gardenias pleased her, yet her heart ached with memories. The courtyard was the only place she could bear to bury her treasure.

Her only regret was that she could not tell her family back in England where she was hiding it. The risk of putting the hiding place in writing, and chancing discovery was too great. However, her nephew, Thomas was an educated gentleman. He would surely be able to interpret the cryptic words she had penned in her diary.

Josephine kneeled in the centre of the pavers and bit her lip as the pain shot down her leg. Carefully placing the precious parcel on the ground beside her, she closed her eyes until the pain eased, and raised a shaking hand to wipe the perspiration from her eyes. Earlier in the day she had innocently placed a small wooden-handled dibber in her gardening basket next to the wrought iron gate and instructed the slave who laboured in the garden to leave the small spade beside the fountain. It was not unusual, as Josephine had spent many hours in the garden over the past five years. Since Francois and Ivan had died, her garden, her memories, and visiting the cemetery had filled her days.

The pavers in the centre of the ornate indoor garden were spaced more widely than those around the outside edge and she leaned forward, testing the movement of them with her fingers. The brick moved a little and she sighed with relief as she reached for the dibber.

This garden held many precious memories for her, and it was not only the privacy that had led her to choose it as a safe place to hide her parcel. The first time she had seen Ivan, she had been on her knees tending this very garden. Francois had frowned at the sight of his wife on her knees digging in the dirt like a slave. When she had become aware he was not alone on that fateful day, she had lifted her gaze to meet the hooded eyes of the dark-haired man standing beside her husband.

A sob caught in her throat as she pushed the narrow end of the dibber beneath the paving brick and lifted it slowly. She picked it up and turned it over and placed it on the low wall of the edge of the fountain in front of her. Not even the worms writhing in the soil could distract her from her mission.

She must ensure it was well hidden. Josephine held scant regard for what may happen to her but she had promised Ivan she would keep it safe. The promise she had made him before he had died had stayed with her, and the events of the past week had confirmed his last words to her.

They will come.

It had been five years, but someone must have finally noticed the necklace that graced her neck in the portrait in La Salle Conde Theatre. Dear Francois had believed it was a family heirloom from her Bellerose great-grandmother, and she had worn it in the portrait he had commissioned. She'd not been able to disillusion him with the truth.

For two hours she toiled through the still of the night. By the time she had removed the pavers and dug a deep hole, the skin on her fingers was rubbed raw and bleeding, and burning pain sliced through her back. Finally, the hole was deep enough, and she set the small spade aside.

Easing up slowly from her haunches, she straightened, taking in deep breaths until the pain faded. The parcel sat on the ground next to the dibber but Josephine couldn't bring herself to pick it up yet, knowing it would be the last time she would see it. The final connection to Ivan would be broken. A deep ache, which was not physical, filled her chest and her vision clouded with unshed tears. She brushed them away impatiently.

I have the rest of my life to shed tears.

She moved slowly across to a large bentwood chest near the door where she had made her preparations earlier in the week. The leather straps came away easily and she reached in for the ceramic crock and lifted it out. She carried it carefully across to the low wall next to the fountain and removed the stopper, before reaching in and retrieving the small Welsh tin box that Francois had brought home from one of his trips to Philadelphia. It fitted into the bottom of the crock perfectly.

Josephine turned to the parcel and stared at it for a long while, before opening the wax-coated linen cloth. She allowed the tears to fall as she slowly pushed the stiff fabric aside while the merry tinkling of the water seemed to mock her sadness.

At last everything was ready. She would allow herself one last look before she wrapped the cloth around it, ready to place it inside the crock and bury it deep beneath the pavers. Spreading the cloth on the low wall beside the fountain, she arranged the contents in the circle which had graced her throat in years gone by.

As Josephine stared down, the clouds cleared the moon through the magnolia tree above and a dazzling rainbow danced across the trickling water of the fountain as a necklace of twenty-eight brilliant emeralds surrounded by a myriad of diamonds caught the light from the full moon.

Chapter One
New Orleans
September 1796

Even after a decade at sea, Sébastien Leclerc was no closer to understanding the appeal of living on the ocean. Unlike his crew, who understood becoming a sailor meant uprooting their life and spending most of their time at sea, Sébastien was not enamoured with a mariner's life. Because of the lucrative rewards, it attracted a mix of men who seemed to ignore the high risk of ending up on the bottom of the ocean floor.

One more mission, one last intercept, and Sébastien's dream of going to Hawaii to start his own sugar plantation would come to fruition. Over the years the guilt he had borne for Lisette's death had lessened, and Sébastien accepted that his actions had merely been those of a young man in love...or lust. Lisette's father had been a wealthy sugar merchant, and she had been spoiled with everything she could want in life— except her independence. She had enticed Sébastien to assist her in her quest to flee her stern father. Sébastien's desire had blinded him to the dangers of a young woman walking alone through Santo Domingo in the dead of night. He had agreed to meet her at the wharf to travel to New Orleans, but she had been kidnapped before he had arrived. It was believed she had been taken by one of the pirate captains in the town and her father had held him responsible.

One more mission, one more month and if all went to plan, his life would change. He would be away from this life where he witnessed servitude and despair every day. One thing Sébastien promised himself, his plantation would be worked by free men. Maybe, just maybe, the scars of the past, and Lisette's fate would leave him, and he could settle and raise a family.

Time heals. Sébastien closed his eyes. He could almost hear the voice of Lucy, the old, dark-skinned cook on their plantation back in Santo Domingo. When Lisette had been taken by the slave traders as she had waited for him at the harbor, and had died on the vessel, he had thought his own life had come to an end. His poor choices as a very young man had led to the death of the young woman he'd loved.

As the winter months drew closer, the increasing cold of the salt-laden breeze warned of the icy winds which would follow. It was time to take safe haven in the harbor and embellish his reputation in the taverns along the Mississippi delta where his half-brother, Jean-Luc, ran the headquarters of the family commercial business in the Rue Royale in New Orleans. It was also well past time to pay his brother a visit; he had avoided him on his past two stays in port. Sébastien was close to having enough gold put away to escape this duty he loathed.

A visit, one more mission and freedom to pursue his own life.

A sudden gust snapped the sails and the pungent aroma of damp wood surrounded him. Closing his eyes for a brief moment he longed for a breeze free of salt, and ground that stood firm beneath his feet.

"Captain?"

Sébastien opened his eyes and swivelled around. The soft voice of one of the slaves they had seized from a British slave trader this voyage interrupted his musing. "You have turned the ship to the land?"

Sébastien nodded. "Yes, it is time to trade our cargo."

"And what of us?" The man's voice was uncertain. "Shall we be traded also?"

Sébastien shrugged and looked the man up and down. There were fifteen slaves on the ship and none knew the true purpose of his business. They assumed they would be put to work on one of the sugar plantations in Louisiana.

To all onlookers, apart from his crew, Sébastien was a river captain, plying his trade between the sugar plantations on the Mississippi River. The presence of slaves on his vessel when they berthed fuelled the rumours that the Leclerc brothers were somehow involved in the slave trade. No one knew of their true business apart from the governor and his aide-de-camp. Even Jean-Luc was not privy to the details of the missions of the vessel he owned jointly with his half-brother. Secrecy was of the essence and the impact of their successful forays was beginning to be felt.

He'd heard the rumours. The latest scuttlebutt from the taverns on the Louisiana coast explained the occasional disappearance of their trader from the regular river trade. They told of Sébastien and his crew marauding the seas between the Delta and the Gulf, seizing bounty as they went; both cargo and slaves, and trading the bounty once they got to the colonies. It was far from the truth and the slaves they rescued as they plied their trade to the British West Indies were either sent back to Africa, or given a choice as soon as they docked in New Orleans. It was a town where those of coloured, quadroon and mulatto heritage lived. Sometimes they chose to stay on his vessel and work the sugar trade. Under the new Spanish law called *coartación*, they could even buy their freedom. It was the least he could do to end the slave trade he abhorred.

The problem was Jean-Luc, his half-brother, who was more concerned with increasing his wealth than worrying about the fate of a few men...slaves or otherwise. Jean-Luc was the progeny of a brief, illicit liaison Sébastien's mother had tried to hide. Jeannie, their mother, had told the truth about Jean-Luc's father on her death bed, but Jean-Luc had been raised in the household in San Domingo.

Much to Sébastien's disgust, the slave trade in Louisiana had become more lucrative over the past few months due to the growth of the cotton plantations after the invention of the cotton gin and he doubted whether Jean-Luc would agree to him keeping these fifteen men on his ship. They had refitted the two-hundred-ton Spanish square rigger during the last stay in Barataria Bay and it was in need of more crew. It would suit him well to take on some more strong men, if they were willing to work for him. He was intending to have a frank discussion with the Spanish governor about the nature of Jean-Luc's intentions. He had a meeting with Carondelet this very night and he knew the intelligence he had to report would not be well received.

In the meantime, he must sort the current situation and placate his brother. Of prime importance was the retrieval of the money owing to him by both the governor, and his half-brother, before the inevitable falling out with Jean-Luc.

Now the man in front of him stood still and straight and bowed his head respectfully. His African black skin glistened in the sunlight. Sébastien narrowed his eyes. He never trusted; who knew what this man had heard.

"And what would you have me do with you and your friends?" It was an opportunity to embellish his reputation. The more people who were wary of him and his crew, and wondered about their true activities, suited him. "Mayhap I am in need of a strong crew when we continue our travels? There are some fine ships filled with enticing cargo down in the Gulf. Perhaps you would prefer to stay on my ship than toil in the sugar fields of the colonies?"

The merchant ship they had seized had been en route to England, and he had generously allowed it to continue after removing a little of its sugar cargo as well as the fifteen slaves.

"Yes, we are strong and the '*Maiden*' is a beautiful ship." The man lifted his head and held his gaze.

"Your language is of a high standard for a captured slave?" He frowned at the African man.

"My friends and I were merchants in Accra on the Gold Coast, but we were kidnapped by the rogue slave traders. They gave no thought to who they captured. As long as they fill their slave markets with men who are strong and can toil, they pay no heed."

Sébastien's interest was piqued. "So how did you get on the British ship and arrive in the American colonies?"

The tall man looked at him without answering and Sébastien turned away. It was bad enough for the man that he was here away from all he knew. He would interrogate him no further.

Good Christ, he hated this slave trade with a passion and the sooner he could end his current intelligence work, the better. Sébastien turned and stared across the prow of the boat as the crew toiled with the sails. Seaman were perched in the rigging and held hands to shield their eyes in the bright sunlight. The command to turn back to Bay St Louis had been issued and they were keen to return to the land, to frequent the taverns.

"Yes, the '*Maiden*' is a fine vessel." He turned away from the man, ignoring his words about his capture. "I shall advise you of your fate when we dock."

Chapter Two

Madeleine Bellerose pressed her fingers to the cool glass of the window and stared out over the green lawn surrounding the family manor. The glass was latticed with diamond panels of soft lead and if she squeezed her eyes half-shut and distorted her vision, she could pretend that the carriage coming across the small bridge at the end of the quarter mile driveway carried Mother and Father home from one of their visits to the nearby village of Danesthorpe. She scrunched her eyes shut to stop the hot tears from sliding down her cheek. Ever since she had been a little girl Father had brought her pretty ribbons from the haberdashers, and Mother would frown and tell him he spoiled his only daughter. Now that she was a young woman, Madeleine had still enjoyed his loving gifts.

Mother would sit beside a cheery fire with her in this room, and they would admire the silken lengths of ribbon as she helped

Madeleine wind them through her hair. She turned away as the carriage wheels clattered as it crossed the wooden bridge and her footsteps echoed through the cold, bare room. The fireplace was full of grey ash and the furniture had been sold. All that remained was her bed. She would never forgive her uncle for clearing her possessions along with everything else in Bellerose Hall

"Madeleine!" The harsh voice of Uncle Titus came from the end of the hall and she paused in mid-step. "Where are you? Edward Phillips' carriage has crossed the bridge and he will wish to meet you."

Madeleine hurried over to the long window on the western side of the room, taking care to step on her toes, so the soles of her shoes did not make a sound on the wooden floor. She slipped behind the burgundy velvet drapes and held her breath. She had no interest in speaking with her uncle or meeting with Edward Phillips, the representative of the society, who was organizing their journey.

"Are you in there, Madeleine?" The angry tones of her uncle's voice reached her and she stood perfectly still as he paused in the doorway. "That girl is in need of a firm hand." The muttering of her uncle faded as he strode to the other end of the long corridor on the first floor of the manor. Whatever he did was always in anger. His voice, his walk and his attitude to her showed his displeasure with his earthly life.

Even the way he eats. He shared no qualities with her dear father, his older brother.

Madeleine had to endure watching Uncle Titus devour his food each night. Worse still, since he had dismissed all of the staff after Bellerose Hall had been stripped, she'd had to prepare his food. She sighed and turned to the window. At least, he'd not been able to destroy the beauty of the garden, and she wiped the tears from her eyes before pushing the casement open, taking in a deep breath of the fresh, cool air. Autumn was not far off but she would not see the leaves fall from the trees this season if Uncle Titus had his way.

The summer garden, planned by her mother with Jed, the Bellerose gardener, was in full-blown beauty as the season drew to a close. The mauve and purple hollyhocks almost reached the oak window pane beneath her fingertips. Scarlet poppies nodded their cupped heads and the fragrance of the pink climbing rose drifted in on the soft afternoon breeze. If she stretched forward she would see the purple wisteria that covered the walls around the main entrance beneath the north-west tower, but she did not want to risk being seen by her uncle, or the visitor. Beneath her, a movement on the fountain terrace caught her eye and she smiled. Jed had refused to leave his beloved gardens even after Uncle Titus had dismissed the staff. Now Jed toiled away each day for no stipend from the estate. Madeleine was determined to bring money back to the estate, no matter what it took. The staff would have their positions back and would not end up impoverished and hungry or even worse having to go to the cities to the new factories that her father had said were springing up all over England. It was her duty as the only surviving member of the Bellerose family. Apart from Uncle Titus who seemed to have more care for strangers on the other side of the world, than the villagers and estate workers who had spent their lives toiling for the family.

It was her duty and she had made a promise on the coffins of her family at the combined funeral for her parents and her brother.

Madeleine lifted her skirts, walked quietly to the door and peered into the long, dim hallway. There was neither sight nor sound of Uncle Titus. He would be down greeting his guest at the front of the manor. She moved quickly along the wide hall, down through the kitchens, picked up two large apples on the way and slipped through the scullery door, past the chapel and out into the gardens. Jed was clipping the full-blown roses, and the perfume of the fallen petals was sweet.

"Is he out here, Jed?" She wanted to make sure that Uncle Titus didn't see her disappear into her secret place. The old man straightened and shook his head.

"You know you can't blame your uncle for what has happened."

"I know that Father was struggling with the upkeep of the estate before he died." She sighed. "Why is it that our family is jinxed? First Grandpapa died when he fell from his horse, and then Uncle Arthur died in London and it was up to my dear father to try to keep it going—" she swallowed as her breath hitched "—and then to lose my parents and my darling brother in that carriage accident."

She swiped angrily at the tears. "I will go to the new world and I will find the heirloom and I'll come back to England loaded with riches and it will all be the same as it was."

Jed patted her arm. "The heirloom? What heirloom? Miss Madeleine, you know you cannot restore the past. Wealth alone won't bring things back to the way they were."

'I must do something to bring money back

to the hall, so the villagers can come back to work. I have found a way to do it. This Hall has been in the family for three hundred years and it will be filled with happiness and laughter again."

"What are you going to do, Miss Madeleine?"

"Do you remember Great Aunt Josephine?"

"Yes, she moved to the American colonies when your father was a young lad."

"She died two years ago. I found her diary in Father's possessions." Madeleine dropped her voice and leaned closer to the old gardener, despite there being no one else to hear them. "And in the pages she writes of a family heirloom. Her own words. All I have to do is go to New Orleans and bring it home to Bellerose Hall and then everything will be all right."

Jed tutted and shook his head. "And how are you going to that? How will you know where to find it?"

"I am still making plans. Great Aunt Josephine has hinted in her diary where it is hidden." Madeleine looked into the distance. The setting sun was shining on the soft-coloured Derbyshire sandstone of the hall, bathing it in a pink glow. "I will find it. But I must set out with Uncle Titus on this journey, as I have no money to go alone. It is fortuitous that the ship will berth in New Orleans." She gave a bitter laugh. "Perhaps if Uncle Titus knew why I am happy to go to America with him, he would say it was God's will."

The old man pursed his lips and she patted his arm.

"It will be all right. Do not worry." She glanced around the gardens and up to the windows that overlooked them but there was no sign of her uncle.

"If he comes out, you have not seen me." She smiled at him and lifted her skirt as she headed for the huge oak tree which was her secret place for reading the diary.

###

Great Aunt Josephine had begun each entry with the date and the weather and had used the early entries simply to record her personal accounts and those of the household accounts of the grand house on Toulouse Rue in New Orleans. Madeleine had been fascinated by the different style of living in New Orleans. Josephine had written vivid descriptions of the visitors to their home, including the fur traders her husband Francois had dealt with each season. Russians, Spanish, French and many other nationalities resided in or plied their trade in New Orleans, yet Madeleine was surprised that Great Aunt Josephine did not appear to have any female acquaintances.

The strange entry soon after the description of a dinner party had caught Madeleine's attention three weeks ago.

His arms encircled me, and my heart swelled with love.

From that curious entry, the descriptions changed from household and social, to personal. Madeleine had taken every opportunity to read the diary. Her cheeks had burned as Josephine had described her meetings with a lover. At first, the language had confused her.

What new passions will my lover find me today? What pleasures unheard of, undreamed of? I crave release in the days he is away from me. I catch my breath and throb with need as I wait for his skilful touch.

She had spoken of meeting him at the cemetery gate near the house and talked of gathering plants with him in the swamp.

And then the words of what they had done!

Unfamiliar feelings had coursed through Madeleine's body as she'd read the description of a physical act of which she knew little. She'd crossed her legs as warm pressure had filled her lower belly. Mother had hinted of the act of union between a man and a woman and had promised to tell her more when she became engaged. But Mother was gone and would never be able to share that knowledge.

Uncle Titus had asked Cook to come back to help prepare one meal for their guest, and yesterday morning, before Madeleine had helped Mrs. Jennings in the scullery, she had snatched a few moments in the library to read the next pages. The diary had drawn her in and she was living through Josephine's words. Excitement had run through her veins yesterday when she had reached a page where an inked drawing of an emerald necklace had filled the page.

Your emerald beauty shall never fade, though the curse of lust may forfeiture love.

What could that mean, lust and love? For the first time, Madeleine realised the lover in the diary may not be Great Uncle Francois. Some pages were harder to read, where the flourishing writing was smudged as though liquid had been spilled or perhaps the writer had shed tears on the words as they had been written.

But the more Madeleine read, the more she was certain that her great aunt had been given a precious necklace and had hidden it. Perhaps it had been from a lover? Father had certainly never mentioned a family heirloom and the diary had been in his possessions. It had been fortunate that she had found it before Titus, and Madeleine had kept it either in her reticule or hidden in the library. If Uncle Titus found out what she was reading, he would lock her away in her room, but she was fascinated by the feelings Josephine had recorded in her diary. Uncle Titus took no pleasure from even the mundane and would be horrified by the sensual words now firmly fixed in her mind.

But more important to Madeleine was the necklace. Cryptic references near the drawing spoke of emeralds and diamonds, and untold wealth. It would mean the resurrection of Bellerose Hall.

Where was it? It must be in Josephine's house in New Orleans. In Rue Toulouse, near a cemetery. Madeleine wondered who the house had been bequeathed to when Aunt Josephine had died. Her great aunt had had no children and her possessions had filled the two small boxes that had been returned to Bellerose Hall just before her parents had been killed. Perhaps Father had not had a chance to look at the diary, so it had never been discussed. Madeleine tried to remember the stories he had told about his aunt, but they wouldn't come.

Perhaps I am the only person in the world

who knows of this hidden necklace?

Madeleine frowned as she tried to decipher the words. Beneath the drawing, a heavy black line of ink crossed from one side of the page to other, perhaps in an attempt to gain a reader's attention?

Safe at rest, at home. In the water, by the water, in the garden. The words crossed the page like a fine gossamer web. Light spidery writing that was almost invisible. The next time she read the diary she would transcribe the words onto another page in case these continued to fade.

It was her only chance and until then, she would memorize them. Over and over she read them, imprinting them into her memory.

But they made no sense. Madeleine turned to the next page searching for more clues. But there were none. She would have to decipher what she had read.

Safe at rest, at home. In the water, by the water, in the garden. That was the clue.

"There you are!"

Madeleine jumped, and the diary slipped from the folds of her skirt as she sat up, and she pushed it deeper into the stiff fabric.

"Come down here, immediately." Uncle Titus was beneath her and his expression was furious. "And hand me whatever it is you are trying to hide."

Chapter Three
New Orleans
September 1796

Doom and gloom stories of pirates from Jake, the ginger-haired cabin boy Madeleine had befriended soon after their departure from Bristol, were the only interesting things she experienced during the journey to the American colonies. The trip had been dull and non-eventful as the sun had moved across the cloudless sky in a monotonous pattern for days. The weather had been kind but despite that, Madeleine was one of the few passengers who had not suffered from the sea sickness. She had enjoyed the gentle rocking in the long lazy swells as they had crossed the ocean. A month of fair weather and good wind had made for a quicker journey than Uncle Titus had anticipated, but the daily prayers as Uncle Titus had droned on above deck each morning had at least given a structure to the day. Madeleine spent most of the daylight hours sitting on the poop deck planning how she would elude her uncle as soon as they made land in New Orleans. Talking with Jake had expanded her vocabulary and she now considered herself quite an expert on nautical terms.

Uncle Titus had taken the diary from her and thrown it back into the library after he had ordered her down from the tree. When she had gone looking for it the next day, she could not find it amongst the thousands of books lining the walls. She'd scanned the shelves and had pulled many books out in a last, desperate bid to locate the precious book.

She'd had no success, but the words she had read were imprinted on her mind. She had no intention of going to the British West Indies with her uncle and had already set aside the only things she wanted to take with her. Some pieces of her mother's jewelry, which she would have to sell, and the favourite ribbon her father had given her.

"Aye, they were a lusty mob." Jake's latest pirate story brought her back to the present. The brigands roamed the seas they were travelling across and were, according to Jake, in search of gold and attractive young women. "The last ship I was aboard had its cargo of jewels and gold purloined, and the captain and the crew each chose a woman to be their doxies on the pirate ship. I have heard Sébastien Leclerc is the most feared pirate from Louisiana to the Caribbean."

Madeleine yawned. Jake's stories had become more bloodthirsty each day and she did not believe one word he said.

Fancy, pirates and doxies. She was aware of the slave trade. Goodness, she had heard Uncle Titus speak for hours of the society he belonged to. He had something to do with the plan to abolish slavery and had forced her to attend a lecture with him in Danesthorpe soon after her family had been buried. It was another reason she loathed her uncle. He had had no consideration for her grief and had told her she should accept her loss as God's will.

At the meeting a man had spoken of the inhuman and immoral treatment of enslaved Africans committed in the name of slavery and was garnering support for a campaign in favour of a new law to abolish the slave trade and enforce it on the high seas. It was the first inkling she'd had that Uncle Titus was planning a voyage.

Slavery and piracy on the high seas was a long way from her life at Bellerose Hall and Madeleine had not given it another thought until Jake had started to tell her the pirate stories.

She was more afraid of having to stay with her Bible-thumping zealot of an uncle than encountering pirates or slave traders.

"So how do I know when we are near a pirate ship?" She decided to humour Jake. He had been a good friend to her on this boring voyage.

Jake looked at her scornfully. "Why, by their black flag, of course."

"Maybe, I might run away from my uncle and join a pirate ship." Madeleine watched a flock of gulls fly over the main sail. Jake knew a little about her situation and how much she loathed her uncle. She had told him of her parents and her older brother and had learned of him being orphaned in London and his own plans to be the master of a ship one day.

'Tis a shame I am not a man. I could make my fortune as a seafarer and travel home when I become rich.

Madeleine sighed and moved across to the side of the boat. Jake followed her. Uncle Titus was asleep. He suffered badly from the sea sickness. Once the daily prayers and Bible reading were done, he disappeared below deck and slept the rest of the day. This had given Madeleine unexpected freedom on the voyage from Bristol.

"Look!" Jake pointed past her just as the cry "Land-Ho" came from the rigging above. "We are almost there. That's the delta of the Mississippi River over there to the west. Now we have to wait out here for a favourable wind and tide to get up to New Orleans."

A lightness filled Madeleine's chest as the prospect of escape and the beginning of her quest came within reach. She grabbed Jake's hands and did a jig around the deck, her bonnet slipping sideways, giving no regard to who may be watching as the sea gulls squawked above them. As soon as they had moored, and she prayed Uncle Titus would not wake, she intended to slip off the ship. She had no idea where she would go, but she would find somewhere safe. A couple of gold coins and her mother's necklace would hopefully pay her way when she found lodgings.

Tonight. I will be alone and I can find out where Aunt Josephine's house is.

She would not spend one day more with Uncle Titus. A niggle of doubt tugged at Madeleine as she worried that the opportunity would not come, or she would not find a hiding place in the town. She knew her uncle. He was determined and would not be bested by a mere slip of a girl.

From this moment, she would pay close attention to the land they passed, especially as they came close to New Orleans. Breathlessly, she dropped onto a water keg on the side of the deck and smiled up at Jake. He had been kind to her over the past month and she would miss him.

"Tell me about New Orleans. Have you been there before?"

"Yes, we have traded sugar from there since I was taken onto this vessel as a cabin boy." He puffed his chest out. "I'm going to be a ship master one day, you know."

"Not a pirate?" Madeleine smothered a grin as he glared at her. "So, tell me, is it like London?"

Jake regarded her scornfully but there was patience on his voice. "It is a town nothing like home. A lot smaller than London, but more streets than the villages we are used to."

Madeleine was tempted to seek Jake's assistance and tell him of her plan to escape. He seemed to know the town and she would have to find a very good hiding place so Uncle Titus couldn't find her. If it was a small settlement, it may be difficult to find her way. A young woman on her own, not knowing the streets around the town, would be fair game for the fur trappers, pirates, and slave traders that

Jake had spoken of.

Madeleine frowned as she considered her options. If she had Jake as an ally, he could perhaps tell her uncle that she had fallen overboard while he was asleep and had not resurfaced.

And then Uncle Titus wouldn't even look for her.

But no, she could not involve anybody else.

Not yet. She would give it some thought as they approached the settlement ahead. Jake was called to the wheel house by the first mate, and Madeleine grimaced as he received a cuff under the ear. Life at sea was hard and violent, but young Jake seemed to take it in his stride. She moved into the shadows at the back of the boat, clasping her hands to her chest as the land got closer and anticipation filled her.

***

It had taken two days for the *Maiden* to travel across the Gulf of Mexico. His half-brother, Jean-Luc had not been at the outpost in Bay St. Louis and had left word for Sébastien to sail up the Mississippi River to New Orleans. They had replaced their pirate flag with the flag of the Leclerc shipping company before they reached the delta. Sébastien ignored the few ships they had passed in the Gulf. It was time for business, not for privateering. A small frigate flying the British flag was now ahead of them as the incoming tide carried them along the Mississippi River toward New Orleans and its captain paid close attention to the *Maiden* as they passed her.

"Oy, I'll have a bit of that." The raucous comment of one of his crew drew a frown from Sébastien, and he glanced at the object of the crewman's attention. A young woman stood in the shadows at the side of the British frigate, watching the dolphins jumping joyfully in the wake of the boat. A dark bonnet hid her hair and she was clothed in a black dress. As he watched, she lifted her head and caught his gaze.

He lifted a hand and acknowledged her as the boat drew abeam of his vessel. He smiled back as her face lit up in a broad grin. She lifted her hand to return his wave but obviously thought better of it. She dropped her head and turned away. Sébastien caught a quick glimpse of a fair complexion touched with red roses high on her cheeks. At close inspection, her bonnet was black, as was her dress, and he wondered why a woman of such youth would be in mourning. He watched with interest as a tall, thin man in a long dark coat moved from the middle of the deck and grabbed her arm. He was in the dress of a clergyman…more commonly referred to as a devil dodger by his irreverent crew.

"Madeleine, you are not to be above deck." His angry words reached Sébastien as the man pulled her roughly to her feet. "Those sailors are ogling you. It is not fitting for a woman to be looked at by such men. Get below immediately." The man, who he assumed was her husband, had called her Madeleine; his voice had been loud and angry enough to carry across the water. For a fleeting moment, Sébastien regretted not being close enough to intercede on the young woman's behalf. He shook his head and chased away the gallant thought. If her husband had told her to stay below deck, she should have obeyed.

Obviously not a widow, then.

But there was no need to be so rough and manhandle her. Her husband held her tightly as he pushed her toward the middle of the boat where the ladder went below deck. Sébastien's interest was distracted as the first mate called for his attention, and he quickly forgot about the young woman as they prepared to dock.

It took another two hours to reach the final bend in the river and approach the busy port ahead. The wharf at New Orleans was bustling with people as captains prepared to discharge their cargo and passengers. Arrivals and departures of vessels were dependent on the tide of the mighty river as the tide ebbed and flowed and there was always a wait before they could quay. Today seemed busier than most and Sébastien sighed. It would be good to leave this behind him and stand looking over his own fields of sugar, on an island far removed from the bustle of this busy port town. A foreman cracked his whip at a dozen slaves chained together, walking slowly along the edge of the wharf. From the boat to the north of his vessel, dark-skinned men began to emerge into the daylight, their feet and hands still secured with chains and they looked around, their expressions closed as they walked down the gangplank toward the quay. The British frigate was coming in to moor to the south of them and Sébastien smiled to himself. The English rose was back on the upper deck leaning over and watching the activity on the land. There was no sign of her husband. He wondered why a well-dressed woman such as herself was travelling on a British cargo frigate to the colonies.

"Take over from me." Sébastien turned to his first mate and pointed to the small group of slaves standing together at the back of his vessel. "Put them below. I shall decide where they will go later." Pulling off his shirt, he swung himself to the mast and began to climb the rigging. From his vantage point high up the mast, he could see across Decatur Street and into Jackson Square where the governor stayed when he was in New Orleans. He squinted into the lowering sun as the bright light reflected off the river. There was little sign of activity, but the flag was raised, indicating the governor was in residence. Sébastien heaved a sigh of relief. He would have a leisurely meal at one of the taverns and perhaps seek out some female company for the evening after he met with Governor Carondelet. They had been at sea for a few weeks and a decent meal was not the only thing his body required.

"Ahoy, Captain."

Sébastien looked down as his first mate called out to him and pointed up to the rigging above the main top. "The rope is fouled, and we can't pull down the sail."

He gave the first mate a wave and swung himself from the platform, across the ropes, carefully keeping his balance by holding onto the rope above his head as he stepped onto the loose rigging which swayed as it took his weight. Cursing softly beneath his breath, Sébastien looked up to the tangle of ropes above him.

"Holy Mother of Christ, how the hell did

that happen?" He shook his head as he muttered the angry words. He'd be having strong words with the first mate about the slackness of the crew member who was responsible for the state of the rigging. It had been satisfactory last time Sébastien had checked but now, its condition was on the head of the first mate and the crew member who had not paid enough attention to the ropes. The first rule of Sébastien's vessel was the care of the sails. He had been in enough storms at sea to know the danger of rigging that was not well cared for.

Stretching across, he pulled at the knotted tangle until the rough rope burned into his palm. He repositioned his feet and moved closer and gave it an almighty tug and the frayed ends of the tangle let go.

"Look out, Captain!"

As the first mate's shout reached him, the rope beneath his feet moved and Sébastien knew he was going to fall. Twisting his body, he leaped into mid-air to the port side and closed his eyes as he stretched into a diving position. The cold muddy waters of the Mississippi covered his head as he sank beneath the surface and he kicked and swam upward, spluttering as the taste of the mud hit his throat.

Charming. Now he'd have to wash and change into fresh breeches before he went to meet the governor. He looked up and despite his anger at the mess in the rigging, Sébastien grinned as half of his crew peered over the side of the boat at him. The gap-toothed grin of his second mate caught his attention as he looked up at the faces above him

***

Madeleine had shaken off Uncle Titus's arm as he'd shoved her roughly below deck. No doubt he deemed it inappropriate for her to be in the view of the ship full of sailors pulling into the wharf ahead of them. To her relief, she had not endured another lecture as Uncle Titus had gone straight to his bunk and fallen asleep after eliciting a promise that she would stay below deck.

"We are in an unfamiliar land and there may be no other women around." His bulbous nose twitched with distaste at the thought of Madeleine having any freedom.

One of the best things about the voyage had been her uncle's constant sea sickness. Madeleine smothered a smile at the uncharitable thought. Uncle Titus had managed to drag himself to the deck for the daily prayers and the Sunday service but had retreated immediately below decks when his sonorous sermon had finished. Madeleine could have told him that if he'd stayed up in the fresh air, the sickness would have soon passed but it suited her well to have him below deck. Spending the time looking out at the ocean and chatting with young Jake had served her very well. She had planned her escape and intended to put her plan in place as soon as the time was right. She'd given no thought as to what would follow her escape and how she would return to Bellerose, but her determination to succeed in finding the necklace pushed those problems to the side. The first step was to get away from her uncle and make good her escape. *Maybe I am being naïve? Maybe a young woman alone with very little money would find it hard to achieve her goal in this town?* She swallowed and pushed her doubt to the side.

Still, once she came back on deck after her Uncle Titus had fallen asleep, a niggle of doubt tugged at her. She was keen to watch what was happening as the vessel next to their boat moored and unloaded its cargo. It could give her an idea of the direction she would take to get to town. It had nothing to do with wanting to see the handsome sailor who had waved to her before Uncle Titus had grabbed her. His eyes had been full of sympathy and she had felt a sizzling connection with the stranger who had caught her eye.

Unfamiliar warmth had rushed through her belly as he'd smiled and waved at her. He had turned his head and held her gaze across the narrow space between the two boats until Uncle Titus had pulled her away from the side. The sailor was tall and dressed differently than the other crew members on the boat. His chest was bare above his tight breeches and the broad expanse of bronzed skin had set her belly churning.

When she thought about it, it was not uncomfortable, and it was a pleasant sensation. It was the same tense pull above her thighs that had set her legs to trembling when she had read Great Aunt Josephine's diary.

She moved to the aft of the boat, keeping her head down as the crew scurried around to ready the vessel as it moved closer to the wharf. Her bolt hole was on a pile of ropes behind the wheelhouse and it had been a comfortable retreat for her throughout the journey. She lifted her head as she sat with her back against the warm timber but there was no sign of her friend, Jake.

"Look out, Captain."

The warning was followed by a loud splash and Madeleine jumped to her feet and ran to the side of the boat. Her fingers gripped the smooth timber as she craned forward looking into the dirty water. She jumped and put her hand to her chest as the water swirled in front of her and a sleek head broke the surface. Raucous laughter drifted across the narrow gap between the edge of the boat she was gripping and the vessel that was about to moor behind it.

"Fancy a dip, did ya, cap'n?" Half a dozen crew members lined the edge of the deck, pointing at the figure in the water. "And you have a pretty lady watching too!"

Madeleine didn't have time to retreat to the shadows before the man turned and looked up at her. His black hair was plastered to his head, and his eyes were full of laughter. White teeth flashed in a tanned and ruggedly handsome face.

Oh my goodness, it's the man who waved to me. He's the captain, no less.

She inclined her head graciously and stepped back into the shadows of the wheelhouse as he treaded water and kept his gaze fixed on her. Her heart fluttered in her chest and she swallowed. Never before had she laid eyes on such a fine-looking man. She sank back into the pile of ropes with her hand on her chest as her heart beat a tattoo in her chest.

The laughter and ribald comments continued and she watched from the shadows as he swam toward the boat. A rope was thrown down to him and Madeleine gasped as he pulled himself up the side of the boat. Strong muscular thighs were outlined by his wet breeches and water droplets ran down his bare back. His muscles flexed as he pulled himself hand over hand up the rope.

"Your uncle is looking for you." Madeleine jumped and looked around as Jake's urgent whisper reached her as he scurried past with his freckled face looking down. She shot him a grateful glance and stood carefully, smoothing her hands down the stiff fabric of her black bombazine mourning dress. She adjusted her bonnet and put a smile on her face as she stepped around the wheel house to face the thunderous look on Uncle Titus's face.

"I instructed you to stay below deck." His voice was cold, and he grabbed her arm.

"I am sorry, Uncle. I was feeling poorly and came above deck for a draught of fresh air."

"Ready yourself. We are going ashore to meet Jeremiah Benjamin, your future husband,"

"My what?" Cold dismay filled her chest.

"You are to marry Jeremiah and travel with him to Antigua. The Lord has spoken to me and I shall be leaving you with him as I go to minister to the heathens."

"I will not."

Uncle Titus held her arm tightly and Madeline winced as he lowered his face to hers.

"You will. We are to meet him in the town. I do not wish that he witness your disobedience." Her arm burned from where his fingers pressed through the stiff fabric of her dress. The captain has kindly allowed us to sleep on board tonight to save seeking lodgings in town."

"Yes, Uncle Titus." Madeleine kept her voice meek as her stomach burned with anger. How could a man be so different from his brother? She blinked away the tears that filled her eyes as she thought of Father. He would have been horrified to see how Uncle Titus treated her.

But only for a few more hours. Soon she would make good her escape. When they went ashore she would look around to seek the best way to elude her uncle…and her intended husband.

***

Sébastien glanced up at the British frigate moored beside his vessel. He knew his square rigger looked out of place in the river beside the sloops and the flat boats of the river traders and was sure he gained extra interest from those who knew what his vessel was capable of.

But not for much longer.

It had been a difficulty mooring for the frigate beside his vessel as the tide had raced past, and the captain had had to send for a large flat boat to pull them in with ropes. One of the African slaves had stood next to Sébastien as the dozen men had grunted and rowed the flat boat until the frigate was pulled in close to the quay. A glimmer of a smile had crossed the dark-skinned face and he'd commented most ungraciously on the talents of the captain of the British vessel. Sébastien had shot him a curious look. The man's knowledge had surprised him throughout the voyage.

After a last order to the first mate to keep the crew on board—and sober—until he returned, Sébastien strolled down the gangplank. The afternoon shadows were lengthening and the number of boats crowded side-by-side made the wharf area even darker. As soon as he reported to the governor, and he found out the details of his very last mission— he allowed a brief smile to cross his face—he would seek some pleasure in the town. He picked his step up a pace and jumped off the end of the timbered plank, watching out for the mud that had been churned up by the traffic on the wharf that day.

Sébastien looked curiously at the British frigate. It was still not secured to the quay and two crewmen were bringing down the sails. A young cabin boy gave him a cheery wave from the aft deck and Sébastien grinned back at him.

Someone else who was pleased to see the shore. It was damn good to have his feet on land again.

There was no sign of the young woman who had looked down at him in the water. A pretty blush had stained her high cheekbones, almost as dark as the rosy red of her pretty lips. He would seek out one of his female acquaintances in the tavern tonight. If the reaction of his body to a pretty woman, despite the chill of the river water, was any indication, the pleasure of a warm soft body against his was long overdue.

But first things first. The governor would have had word by now that his boat was moored at the quays and he needed to make his way to the meeting.

***

"Tonight?" Sébastien stared at Governor Carondelet, dismayed by the instruction he had just been given, yet delighted that his last mission was imminent. "Francisco, as much as that suits me very well, my crew will be rebellious if they do not have at least one night on land."

Governor Carondelet flicked a speck of imaginary dust off the waist-length satin waistcoat beneath his cutaway tailored coat. "Time is of the essence, Sébastien." The governor's delicate eyebrows were raised in surprise; he was obviously taken aback that a mere ship's captain would challenge him, no matter the successful intelligence work that Sébastien had done for him for the past two years. The governor's time in the Spanish-held settlement had been busy as he had attempted to thwart the Americans from trying to secure unchallenged access to the Mississippi River. But, since the Treaty of San Lorenzo had established a friendship between the United States and Spain and defined the boundaries of the United States with the Spanish colonies, Carondelet's attention had now turned to the slave trade which he abhorred as much as Sébastien.

"It has been reported that the British trader, the Ann Marie is heading to Barbados, loaded with slaves, and it is without an escort." The governor's smile was bland. "We can take advantage of the attention that the British navy is now paying to the French on the seas. The Ann Marie can be intercepted before she reaches the West Indies. But you only have ten days, before it is too late. They departed the Gold Coast of Africa six weeks ago."

"And what shall I do with the cargo?"

"I will leave that to you, for the time being, Sébastien." The governor crossed to the ornate oak sideboard and lifted the decanter of port. The golden liquid caught the candlelight as he removed the cut glass stopper. "I have more concerns with the fear of a further rebellion in Louisiana since the new slave code has been introduced. The slave owners are, shall we say, less than enamoured of me at the present time."

"Slave code?" Sébastien had not heard of this. "When did that happen?"

"Since the French abolished slavery two years ago, the local plantation owners have been vocal, as they fear for the cotton industry as well as the sugar production. I have formed three companies of people of African descent and there are now prescribed standards for quantity and quality of food and clothing for the plantation slaves."

"That is wonderful news." Sébastien took the glass of port and swirled the liquid around in the glass before taking a sip. "You are aware this is my last mission?"

The governor nodded. "Yes, I am and I wish you well in your venture to the Hawaiian Islands.

Sébastien's head flew up and the governor smiled at him over the rim of his glass. "I have spies everywhere, Captain, and please do not fear, I know of your concern with your brother. Your gold is safe. I have ensured that for you, in appreciation of the fine work you have done for me." Carondelet crossed to the window as the last rays of the setting sun hit the glass. "I fear that it will be a long time before the king can…it will be a long time before the slave trade is abolished in all the dominions of Spain. In the meantime, I, and your vessel, shall play our small parts."

"One more request, Francisco." Sébastien crossed to the window and looked out over Jackson Square with the governor. "I have fifteen slaves on my vessel now and they are educated men. I suspect they may be of great assistance on this last mission." He levelled his gaze at the man beside him. "With your permission, I would like to take them with me on this voyage."

"I trust your judgment." The governor put his hand on Sébastien's shoulder. "I wish you a safe voyage and pray that you will return without mishap. His eyes twinkled as he smiled. "I am sure you will be departing for your islands soon."

***

Her intended husband was a short, fat man with lank hair and sour breath. When he had taken her hand in his, it had reminded her of one of the cold, floppy fish that she and her brother had caught in the brook below Bellerose Hall when they were children.

"I am indeed honoured to take you as my wife." Jeremiah Benjamin's rank breath brushed her face as he leaned in close, and Uncle Titus frowned at Madeleine as she snatched her hand away and stepped back. They stood in the shadows beneath a balcony of a building in a street not far from the wharf.

"I have booked the church for tomorrow morning and have arranged for you to conduct the ceremony, Titus."

Her uncle nodded. "I shall depart on the tide in the afternoon and leave you with your new wife."

Madeleine's stomach roiled as Jeremiah turned to her. "I have taken the liberty of securing a room in the town for our wedding night."

Over my dead body. No way would she marry this horrid man. No way would she marry anybody.

"Uncle Titus, may I ask you for something that is very dear to my heart?" She kept her voice meek and hurried on as her uncle's eyes narrowed. "Before we go back to the ship, may we take a walk through the town and see where Great Aunt Josephine lived?"

He stared at her without speaking for a long moment. Madeleine waited. It would be so much easier if she knew where the house was.

"Do you think I am a fool, Madeleine?" A shiver ran down her back as he exchanged a glance with her intended. "I read that…that… filth that my aunt penned in that diary. I had hoped that you had not read it."

"Perhaps I could take Madeleine for a stroll down to the Rue Toulouse?"

Her uncle butted in, but Madeleine stared at Jeremiah, taken aback that he knew the street that the house was on. She narrowed her eyes as she wondered at the connection between him and her uncle. Her uncle had obviously read and shared what had been in the diary.

"No, that would be entirely inappropriate." Titus exchanged a glance with Jeremiah who cleared his throat nervously.

"Of course, of course." His fleshy hand reached out for Madeleine's hand again and she turned away. This time she was not even going to pretend to be polite. As soon as Uncle Titus was asleep she was going to run away. Keeping her head down, Madeleine stepped off the edge of the porch. She let out a soft cry as she stepped straight into the path of a tall man who was striding around the corner. He grabbed at her shoulders as she lost her balance.

"I am so sorry, madam. I was not watching where I was going." His voice was deep, and heat ran up Madeline's neck when she looked up and caught his amused gaze. It was the man from the boat. The one who'd fallen in the water. The man who had smiled at her and had made the heat run through her body.

"Madeleine." Uncle Titus stepped onto the road and took her arm. "Watch where you are going." He turned to the man with the tanned face. "I am sorry, sir."

The man held his hand up. "No harm done. Good day." He caught Madeleine's eye as she looked past Uncle Titus. The heat ran into her face as he held her gaze a little longer. "Good day, madam."

They took leave as soon as the two men had finalized arrangements to meet at the church in the morning. Uncle Titus escorted Madeleine to the end of the street leading to the boat, but she stopped before they turned the corner. The afternoon was quickly fading into evening and lights were coming on in the buildings. She looked with interest into the windows and open doorways. Everything was so bright and colourful—nothing like the muted colours of Bellerose Hall.

"Uncle Titus?" He was striding along ahead of her and she had to call his name a second time before he turned around with a frown.

"What now?"

Madeleine bit back an angry retort and tried to keep her tone civil. "How is it that Mr. Benjamin knew where Aunt Josephine's house was?"

"It is a small town." He would not meet her eye and a chill ran down her spine. Something was amiss here. "Is Mr. Benjamin a missionary too?"

"He has a sugar plantation in Antigua."

"And you think you can just marry me off to him and abandon me in the wilds of a country far from home?" Anger fuelled Madeleine's words. "And why him? He is a most unpleasant man."

"Enough." His voice was stern.

She pushed her anger away. There was no point getting Uncle Titus upset but she was uneasy about the situation. She dropped her gaze and spoke quietly. "I am sorry, Uncle. I am sure you know what is best."

"Indeed." He waited for her to pass him and Madeleine kept her head down as he walked behind her to the ship, her thoughts crowding her head as she plotted her escape. Maybe this betrothal could work in her favour.

If Uncle Titus thought she was with Mr. Benjamin and her intended husband thought she was safely with her uncle on board this ship, no one would look for her and she would be free to find Great Aunt Josephine's house.

Chapter Four

It was stuffy below decks and the air was rancid. The privy in the corner had not been attended to since they had departed Bristol and Madeleine gagged as the stench wafted across to her. The captain had allowed Jake to rig up a curtain of sorts to give her privacy, but it did not mask the smell. No wonder Uncle Titus was ill all of the time. It was not sea sickness, it was the malodorous stench that came from the excrement in the corner. She sat quietly on the edge of the bunk, her mind darting here and there as she waited for Uncle Titus to fall asleep and begin snoring.

After what seemed an eternity, the soft snuffling preceded a trembling snore.

"Uncle Titus?" she whispered.

No response.

Madeleine held her breath as she stood and crept over to his bunk.

"Uncle Titus?" She made her voice a little louder, but still he didn't stir. Quickly, she checked that her reticule was firmly secured to her skirt before she gathered up her soft bag. Madeleine took a last quick look around the cabin she had shared with her uncle for the past thirty-two nights. She crept slowly to the ladder, her breath still held, but now more from the fear of her escape plan being thwarted than to avoid the unpleasant smell.

She had come to a decision in the past few hours. It was the only way she could stop her uncle from pursuing her. Closing her eyes as she climbed the ladder, she prayed that Jake was above deck and had not gone ashore with the rest of the crew. While she had been waiting for her uncle to fall asleep, the clatter of eager footsteps on the gangplank had reverberated through the cabin. Surely, he would not have gone to the taverns?

"Please be there," she whispered to herself. If he was gone, she would have to come up with a new plan.

She stepped from the ladder onto the deck and all was quiet aboard the frigate. Soft voices and the occasional laugh carried across the water from the other vessels, but it appeared that most crews had disembarked and gone into the town. Her heart was thudding in her chest and she was sure it would be heard by anyone who was on deck. A couple of crewmen were on the upper deck, but she crouched low and stayed out of their sight as she crept across to the wheelhouse in the centre of the frigate behind which Jake had a small bed. It had at first horrified her that he had to sleep on the open deck, but he had told her stories of much worse conditions on other boats. Madeleine had realised that her previous life had given her little knowledge of the real world. She had led a very sheltered and well-loved existence.

Her heart beat slowly and heavily as her eyes gradually became accustomed to the dark. She had not ventured on deck after sunset before, even when her uncle had been asleep and snoring. Her hand flew to her mouth as a soft voice came from behind.

"Miss Madeleine? What are you doing?"

She spun around and lowered her hand to her chest to still her fast beating heart.

"Oh, Jake, you startled me," she whispered.

"Why do you have your bag? Are you leaving tonight?" Jake looked around. The young cabin boy whose company she had enjoyed so much and who had made the journey bearable seemed to sense her urgency and kept his voice low. "Where is your uncle?"

Madeleine dropped her bag to the ground and took his hands between hers. They were rough from hauling ropes and scrubbing the decks.

"Jake, I have a considerable request to make of you." Despite her determination, Madeleine's voice trembled. "I beg you to help me."

"You know I'll do anything for you, milady." He gripped her hands between his. "I knew it. You are going to escape from your uncle, is that so?"

Madeleine had shared her discontent with Jake as they'd talked on the long days of the journey. She nodded as a lump lodged in her throat and she pulled away from him and picked up her bag.

"Tell me what you need me to do."

"I am going to leave the boat and I need you to pretend I have jumped overboard." She picked up her bag and pushed it into Jake's hands. "When I am safely on the wharf, I want you to throw this bag into the water and call for help as loud as you can. Rouse Uncle Titus and tell him I was distraught and jumped into the water."

"Are you sure?" Jake looked down at the bag. "What about your possessions?"

"I have everything I need sewn into my dress and in my reticule. I have been doing that each night while he was sleeping."

Madeleine grabbed Jake's shoulders, leaned across and kissed the young man's cheek. "I will owe you for this. When I have found the treasure that belongs to my family, I will seek you out and repay you."

She waited for Jake to cross the deck to the seaward side of the vessel and when he waved to her, she lifted her skirts and headed for the gangplank.

"Madeleine!" Uncle Titus' voice bellowed from below at the same time as she heard the loud splash as Jake threw her bag overboard. She scurried across the deck and ran down the steep timber plank, ignoring the drop to the water on each side. Fear and determination lent her feet wings, and she jumped to the ground, running toward the shadows of the ship moored beside the frigate.

"Madeleine! Where are you?"

"Oh, sir." The plaintive voice of Jake reached her in the shadows where she stood.

"Where is she?" She could not see Uncle Titus high on the boat but his voice was angry. "Where is that disobedient niece of mine?"

"Oh, sir, I fear she is drowned. She pushed by me and climbed up on the side and jumped into the river." Madeleine smiled as Jake's words carried across to her. "She was wild-eyed and crying as she climbed over the side."

Don't overdo it.

"Help us. You, man, find a boat. My niece is in the river."

Madeleine looked around as a flash of light caught her eyes. A man was walking along the wharf swinging a lantern, and it was only a matter of seconds before the light would reach her, showing her whereabouts to anyone who happened to glance down to the wharf. As she turned her head the clatter of feet on the deck of the frigate gave indication that crewmen were taking heed of her uncle and coming to the river's edge to search for her.

With a soft gasp, she grabbed her skirts and ran to the gangplank of the closest vessel. Ducking her head, she ran up the incline until she reached the deck of the unfamiliar boat. Her mouth was dry as she heaved in a deep breath and her legs were trembling with the fear of being discovered. If Uncle Titus found her now, he would lock her away and she would lose any chance of escaping him and completing her quest. If he discovered her, she may as well throw herself in the river.

Crouching down and pressing herself against the side of the hull, Madeleine caught her breath as she looked around. This end of the boat was in darkness, but she could hear men's voices to her left and a soft light shone down from the upper deck. The ruckus on the frigate beside this boat began to grow louder and Uncle Titus' voice was loud—and to her amazement—it was also struck by some emotion other than anger. She tried to ignore the shaking in his voice as it came across the water.

"Oh, dear God, you must help. She is only a slip of a girl."

Three loud splashes reached her, and Madeleine realised that crewmen had jumped into the river to search for her. A pang of guilt ran through her as she worried for their safety in the swirling muddy waters. She would never forgive herself if someone drowned in a futile search for her. A movement on the upper deck of the boat she had boarded caught her attention and a light bathed the deck close by her. She realised that some crewmen from this boat were running toward the lower deck, obviously to assist in the search.

Without thinking, Madeleine ran for the ladder in the centre of the deck which was still in darkness, praying that those searching were still on the upper deck. As her head dipped below the opening, a light passed by and she climbed quickly down the last few steps before jumping soft-footed onto the smooth timber floor. She looked around. A narrow corridor led toward three shuttered doors. It was very different to below-deck on the frigate, which had been comprised of one large space. She and Uncle Titus had shared their lodgings with the small amount of cargo on board while the crew had slept in the forward hold. The light here was dim but it was enough for her to find a temporary hiding place. More footsteps clattered above her head and the loud voices carried down into her hiding space.

"Hurry. Quickly."

"It's the girl from the boat."

"We have to find her. Come on, man. Get the bloody lantern."

The voices dropped, and she couldn't hear what they were saying. Madeleine pressed herself against the hull. Jumbled words which she couldn't decipher until the yelling of the searchers faded away.

"She is the only one who knows where the necklace is hidden. She cannot drown." The urgent whisper made her skin crawl, but Madeleine didn't recognise the voice. Who could it be? She pressed herself hard against the timber and strained to listen, but the voices faded away.

A loud knocking on the timber above her head was accompanied by another shout. "Hoy, wake up. A young woman is in the river."

A creak came from behind the door closest to her and Madeleine gasped. The noise indicated there was someone else below deck. They could not know she was here but she was not going to risk it. Her heart pounded in her chest as she looked around for somewhere to hide. A light shone through the shutters as a lamp was lit and she held her breath as she crept softly to the other end of the short corridor. The other cabins appeared to be in darkness and she had to take a chance that the occupants were either sleeping—or please God—not there.

Swallowing hard, she pushed open the door farthest from the ladder and slipped into the darkness, cocking her head to listen for any movement or sound.

All was quiet.

Gradually her eyes became accustomed to the dark and she looked around. The cabin was large and appeared to follow the hull all the way along to the upper deck.

A large table in the middle of the room was covered with pieces of parchment, but it was too dark to see what they were. She crept silently along the outer wall, her soft-soled slippers making no noise. At the end of the large space was a narrow opening in the timbered hull which would hopefully give her a view of the vessel she had left. As she made her way to the end, she looked around, searching for a hiding place. If anyone came below deck she could hide down here until she could get off the boat and make her way back to the wharf. A wide bed filled an alcove at the very end of the space and Madeleine sighed with relief as she spied a smaller bunk in a small alcove with a curtain across the front. Slowly she pulled it back. The bunk was clear with no bedding and looked as though it was unused. Dropping the curtain down, she made her way over to the narrow fissure and pressed her face against it to see what was happening. Her bonnet was tight against her head and she reached up, removed it, and then unwound the tight braid coiled on the back of her head. She massaged her tense scalp and let out a small sigh of pleasure as her hair tumbled free.

As soon as the activity ceased, and the coast was clear, she would get off this boat and make her way to town. Her first goal had been achieved. She was off the boat and away from Uncle Titus, and that horrid man who she was supposed to marry. It had been relatively easy. Madeleine allowed herself a small smile as she watched the lantern lights play on the fast-flowing waters of the muddy river.

Chapter Five

It was almost midnight by the time Sébastien made his way through the streets from Jackson Square back to the wharf. He'd passed the taverns without a sideways glance and ignored the temptation of a quick drink. There would be time for that when they were under sail later tonight. But perhaps it would not be fair to the crew if he allowed himself the pleasure of a drink, a meal, and the comfort of a soft, warm woman.

And that thought led him to think of the young woman from the frigate. He had been hurrying to meet the governor when she had stepped in front of him and he'd not been able to get her from his thoughts. She had seemed distressed and he wondered what was happening. New Orleans was a small town. He would be sure to find out who she was if they were still here when he returned from his mission.

After Carondelet had left him with the aide, they had plotted the route for his mission. The *Maiden* had to depart in three hours to catch the outgoing tide. Just enough time to sober up the crew who would surely have disregarded his orders and cracked open a keg. The muted voices of his men drifted over to him and the flickering light on the stern cast shadows against the wheelhouse. He stood to the side and let their conversation wash over him. Behind them, the Africans were sitting quietly with their backs to the side of the boat. He had requested of their leader that they look as though they were chained to keep up appearances and they had been strangely acquiescent.

"It was your fault, boy." The distressed wail reached Sébastien as he stood at the top of the gangplank. "You shall pay."

"Ow, let go."

The devil-dodger from the British frigate was striding along the wharf in the darkness, dragging a small boy by the forearm.

"I couldn't stop her." The young voice ended on a wail as the man cuffed his chin.

"Her death is on your conscience." Anger filled the man's voice and Sébastien looked to the side as his first mate joined him at the side of the deck.

"Let. Me. Go." The young high-pitched voice floated up to them.

"What's happening, Mr. Abrahams?" Sébastien turned to his trusted first mate. Despite being a river trader, they followed the seafaring protocols of address.

"The young woman on the British frigate went overboard while you were gone."

"Young woman? The one in mourning dress?" Sébastien frowned. It must be her; that was her husband who was manhandling the cabin boy. His throat tightened and a hollow feeling gripped his gut.

"Yes, we have assisted in the search, but it was called off an hour ago. With the incoming tide, her body will be way up river by now."

Slap! The sound of a fist hitting flesh was followed by a scream as the small lad fell to the ground.

"You will pay. I will ensure you have no position on this boat. I will talk to the captain as soon as he returns." The man in the black coat was almost frothing at the mouth and Sébastien couldn't help himself.

The mistreatment of any human being, of any colour, age or creed, did not sit well with him. A slow anger began to simmer within his chest. "I won't be long." He turned from Mr. Abrahams and ran back down the gangplank to the wharf. The boy was curled on the ground with his hand against his mouth and a trickle of blood ran down from the corner of his eye. Sébastien ignored the man standing over the lad and bent over and lifted him to his feet. The boy appeared to be about thirteen, at most, and his grimy face was wet with tears.

"It weren't my fault." He sniffled and wiped the back of his hand across his face, smearing blood and tears in a long streak down his cheek.

"Leave the boy alone." Sébastien stood in front of the lad as the man lifted his hand.

"Mind your business." The man was wild-eyed and Sébastien knew if he didn't intervene, he would hit the boy again.

He turned to the boy who was creeping away. "Go up on my vessel. My first mate will attend to your face. The boy's eye was already swelling where the man had cuffed him.

He called up to his first mate. "Mr. Abrahams, see to the boy, please."

"Yes, captain." Sébastien waited until the boy had reached the deck. Taking the arm of the angry man, a ripple of distaste shuddered through Sébastien. "I understand you have suffered your wife's loss but—"

"My wife? I have no wife." The man pulled away from him "It is my niece who went overboard. Did she not know it is a sin in the eyes of the Lord to take your own life?"

"I am sorry for your loss but there is no need to take it out on the young boy." Sébastien dropped the man's arm. He had little time for missionaries and their fervour. "I suggest you go back to your boat and have a swig of something to calm you."

The man's cold, dark eyes looked back at him vacantly for a moment before he turned on his heel and walked away. "I will pray for calm, and I will pray for her soul. She was a spoiled young woman from a wealthy family who did not worship our Lord."

Sébastien shrugged and went slowly back up to the deck. It was sad that a life had been lost. It seemed that the man was more concerned with his own state of mind and his niece taking her life than her actual death.

Such a waste. She had seemed like a young woman of spirit. Her face had hovered on the edge of his mind since he had first seen her, and he knew it was one of the reasons he'd intended to lose himself in one of the willing girls on shore tonight. She had made him think of Lisette and it sounded as though she had grown up in a similar privileged family. He wondered briefly why she had travelled with her uncle but soon forgot about her as the first mate beckoned him over.

He was attending to the swollen eye of the young lad who now held a damp rag to his face. Sébastien looked him up and down. "You're a cabin boy, lad?" he asked kindly.

The boy nodded.

"I am in need of a good lad for my next voyage. Are you a good worker? Would you like to join my crew?"

"Oh, yes, Captain. I am one of the hardest workers you will ever find."

He held out his hand and the boy's small hand was almost lost in his grip.

"Welcome to the *Maiden*. My name is Leclerc. Sébastien Leclerc."

Sébastien grinned at Mr. Abrahams as the boy's mouth dropped open.

"Leclerc? Sébastien Leclerc? The pirate?"

Chapter Six

As Sébastien had anticipated, his crew was less than happy with the news that they would be heading out to sea in the middle of that night. A promise of extra grog rations when they restocked the boat at Barataria Bay had placated them to some extent and they got to work setting the sails as they waited for the tide to turn.

"I want our departure to attract as little attention as possible." He instructed the first mate who quietly conveyed the message to the crewmen already climbing the rigging.

Sébastien made his way over to the group of slaves who were sitting on the upper deck and inclined his head for their leader to join him by the side of the deck.

"Those of you who wish to join me will remain on the *Maiden* and assist with this miss—voyage." He held the man's gaze as the lantern light from the crew up in the rigging danced around them. "Those of your group who do not wish to stay on board can disembark at Barataria Bay. But if all goes well, you may be able to join a vessel that will be returning to your homeland."

"I will speak to my brothers." The man left him and Sébastien walked back over to his first mate, glancing down at the new cabin boy who was curled up asleep on the deck.

"See that the young lad has a decent bed for the night." He stared back over to the frigate. "I do not like to see anyone treated so."

###

Two hours later, as the tide slowly turned, the ropes securing the vessel to the wharf were thrown from the bollards and the gangplank quietly raised. Sébastien nodded with satisfaction as the outgoing tide caught them and the lights of New Orleans were left behind as the vessel headed swiftly for the delta on the racing ebb tide.

"A good departure, Mr. Abrahams. Please convey my appreciation to the crew." He let go of the wheel and looked up at the rigging. "I presume the foul in the rope has been attended to?'

"Yes, Captain."

The crewmen on his vessel were a rowdy,

lusty group of men, but he knew that the majority were loyal to him, though a couple of the newer crew who had joined the vessel when they'd stopped at Barataria Bay had yet to prove their worth, as did the Africans.

But Sébastien was satisfied for the most part. Before they reached the Ann Marie he would brief the first mate and he could convey their intentions to the men, but they had a week or so before that would need to happen. Once they left the bay, there was a risk of bad weather. It would be unfortunate if a hurricane were to jeopardize this, his final mission.

Sébastien turned his attention back to the river as they slowed; it was widening as they approached the delta. As soon as they were into the Gulf, he would hand the steering over to Mr. Abrahams and go below deck for some much-needed sleep. He shook his head as he thought of the sad fate of the young woman. Life could be cruel.

***

Madeleine had stood on her toes and peered through the narrow opening in the hull until her legs ached. She leaned down, twisted the back of her skirt into one hand and rubbed the back of each leg in turn. Her muscles burned from standing too long, and she stood and stretched as a yawn overcame her. She cast a glance at the wide bed beside her and dismissed the brief idea of lying down on it. But a quick rest would reinvigorate her for the walk into town, when all was quiet. She stepped over to the alcove where the small bunk was hidden and cast her eye around for something soft to lie on. A coarse woolen blanket, folded into a large square sat atop a small cupboard and she took it down before shaking it and spreading it on the timber on the small bunk. She slipped her shoes off and climbed up and lay there, placing her bonnet beside her. Sleep was not an option, and she would keep her eyes open, so she didn't fall asleep. She would count to one thousand to pass the time and then she would go carefully back on the deck and prepare to leave the boat. Surely, they would abandon the search for her soon?

A loud creak of timber woke Madeleine and she sat up like a shot. She rubbed her eyes and frowned. She must have fallen asleep. Just as she realised that the boat was rocking from side to side, the door to the cabin opened and closed with a soft click. Another creak and her hand flew to her mouth.

It shouldn't be moving so much, wasn't it moored on the river? They had left behind the rocking swells of the ocean when they had turned into the wide river mouth yesterday.

Now she had the same sensation of movement that she'd had on the frigate she'd spent the last month on. And on top of that, she could hear soft noises as someone moved quietly through the cabin, and she held her breath.

Thank the Lord she hadn't given in to the temptation of lying on the wide bed. She would have been in full view of anyone who had entered the room and she certainly would have been discovered by now by whoever was there, even in the darkness of the cabin. If she stayed as quiet as a church mouse, she may be safe. Fear prickled her skin and she clenched her fingers, too frightened to move, almost too frightened to breathe. A lantern spluttered to life and she leaned back as far as she could when a soft light bathed the space and shone through the thin curtain. That was all that there was between her and discovery. A thin piece of material hanging from three brass hooks at the top of the alcove. Now that there was a soft light she could see the space she had hidden in. She glanced down and stifled a groan by biting down on her fingers as she noticed the blanket was hanging below the edge of the bunk, beneath the protection of the curtain. Her gaze settled on her bare toes and she bit down harder. Oh damnation. Her shoes were still on the floor beside the alcove.

A rustling of clothes was followed by the sound of water being poured and she waited.

And waited…and waited.

After what seemed an eternity, footsteps passed by her hiding place and she held her breath as a shadow paused and blocked the light. She lifted her hands to cover her mouth as she waited for the curtain to be pulled aside. But the footsteps continued on, and a further creak was followed by more rustling. He, whoever it was, must have gotten into the bed.

Now all she had to do was wait him out and hope to God that whoever he was, he snored like Uncle Titus and she could soon make her escape. The problem uppermost in her mind, though, was where she would escape to. With each loud creak and rock of the boat, Madeleine became more certain it was no longer moored in New Orleans.

A sneeze tickled her nose and tears filled her eyes as she pinched her nose until it passed. A few moments later her throat tickled, and she swallowed as she fought the need to cough. Minutes passed, and her legs began to cramp again. She had pulled them beneath her as she'd hunched against the side of the hull when the door had opened.

All was quiet, and Madeleine decided it was now or never. Perhaps he had lain with his back to the alcove? Perhaps he had fallen asleep? She had never been overly religious but now she sent a silent prayer heavenward.

Please, Lord, let me get out of this situation. Perhaps she was being punished for pretending to drown?

Slowly and silently, she stretched her legs, taking care not to move the blanket or the curtain. Turning her body so that she was facing the end of the cabin where the bed was situated, she reached for the curtain.

Madeleine closed her eyes tightly as her fingers curled around the thin fabric and fear lodged in her throat like a stone. She listened before she moved the curtain open a tiny distance.

There was no sound.

Opening her eyes, she swallowed down her trepidation and took a deep breath to fortify her courage as she leaned to the left. She moved the curtain a little more and dropped it back with a loud gasp as she encountered the amused stare of a bare-chested man who was reclining on the bed with his hands tucked casually behind his head. His gaze was fixed on her hiding place.

"Unless a ghost has taken residence in my cabin, I presume I am looking at one supposedly drowned niece?" His voice was deep and resonated though the cabin. Despite her predicament a strange feeling ran through her. It was like a shiver but it was warm and pleasant. She ignored the butterflies that were fluttering around in her chest and forced herself to look at him again. When she met his gaze, the warm feeling came flooding back and she cast her eyes down as she lowered her feet slowly to the floor. She searched for her slippers. Perhaps she may yet be able to escape the cabin but she wouldn't get far without her slippers. There was nothing more she could do, apart from throwing herself on his mercy.

Her slippers were nowhere to be seen. Heat filled her cheeks as she lifted her gaze again to meet that of the handsome man who had grinned at her as he'd swum to this very boat. The same man whose hands had gripped her shoulders in the street just a few hours ago. Was she destined to meet him at every turn?

Was it only a few hours ago? It was as though she'd lived a hundred days while she'd been hiding.

Her soft slippers dangled from his fingertips as he pushed himself up from the bed to stand. "I presume you are looking for these?"

He moved closer and Madeleine tried to step away from him, but the hull was already hard up against her back. She lifted her chin and met his steady gaze. Any amusement that may have been on his face had disappeared and his dark eyes pinned hers. She gasped as he raised his hand, but he put it on the wall above her head as he leaned closer.

"Now, although I am very pleased that you are not drowned, perhaps you would like to tell me what you are doing on my boat and more particularly, why you are hiding in my cabin"

"I didn't know it was your cabin." Madeleine kept her voice steady. Every horror story that Jake had told her about sea captains, pirates, and life on board ship crowded her thoughts. The last thing she would do was show him her fear.

She smiled and reached for her shoes dangling by his side. "And if you would kindly give me my slippers back, I will be out of your way and off your vessel."

"You intend to have another swim?" His eyes crinkled with amusement as his gaze bore into hers and she caught her breath. She felt pinned, as though she was like one of the butterflies that were still dancing in her stomach. But it was not fear that she felt. Instinctively she knew he would not harm her.

"Or perhaps you never had one in the first place?"

"What do you mean?" She shook her head as she stared back at him, unable to pull her eyes away from his intent gaze. She'd not taken heed of what he had been saying. All she knew was, his voice was deep and when he spoke his words were tinged with a musical accent which she didn't recognise. He certainly wasn't British, and she had heard no speech like his before. Not that she had had a vast experience in her sheltered life back at Bellerose Hall. His accent reminded her of a French governess who Father had employed to teach her a language when she was much younger, but he sounded his words differently.

She tried to take another step away from him, but he lowered one hand and his fingers curled around her wrist. She stared down at his hand. He wore a large ring on his middle finger and if she wasn't mistaken, it was a ruby as large as a pigeon's egg.

"It will be very hard to leave the *Maiden* and go ashore as we are now approximately ten miles out into the Gulf of Mexico."

Black lights danced behind Madeleine's eyes and she struggled for breath as a cold prickly feeling worked its way from her chest to her throat. "The *Maiden*?" she croaked.

"Yes, the *Maiden*. I am Captain Sébastien Leclerc and the *Maiden* is my vessel."

"Sébastien Leclerc? The pirate?" Madeleine barely had the words out when darkness consumed her and she crumpled to the floor.

Chapter Seven

Were it not for the fact that the woman in his arms was unconscious, Sébastien would have found the soft curves of her body appealing. The stiff black fabric of her mourning gown had hidden the shapely curves which had pressed against him as she'd slid down the front of his body and he'd caught her just before she'd hit the luxurious wool carpet which covered the hard wood of his cabin floor. Now, he reached down and placing one arm below her knees and another beneath her shoulders, he lifted the young woman. A glorious swathe of auburn curls hung over his forearm as he walked across to his bed. He laid her down, letting her slippers drop to the floor with a soft thud.

What the name of God was he to do now? Sébastien stifled a groan of frustration as he pondered his predicament.

He had an unmarried woman in his cabin. An unmarried woman from a wealthy family. A young woman who was believed to have drowned had somehow got onto his boat. He had a little more than a week to intercept the Ann Marie, and that would be his last chance to earn enough to escape this life which he hated more with each passing day. If he turned back to the coast and went back up the Mississippi River to return her to her uncle, there would be no chance of intercepting the slave trader. As it was, they must go via Barataria Bay to reprovision the boat with food and water for the crew. For a brief moment he considered putting her off there in the care of his half-brother, but quickly dismissed that thought. Even if Jean-Luc was at the outpost, he wouldn't trust him to keep his hands off this young woman, and that was also giving no consideration to the wild behaviour he had witnessed in the isolated outpost of the colonies. It was no place for a gentlewoman of class.

A very beautiful young woman. One, by all accounts, who was presumed to have drowned in the river. If her uncle's violent reaction to the cabin boy was any indication of his usual temperament, Sébastien could understand why she might have been trying to escape him.

So, as well as having a beautiful woman on board a vessel which he could not turn back, he did not have the luxury of time to divert from the planned route. On top of that, he had to consider her safety among a lusty crew who had barely seen a woman for months. Three new crewmen, plus young Jake, were on board the *Maiden* for this voyage. He knew he could trust his usual crew to show her due respect, but the new crewmen who they had picked up at Barataria Bay were unknown to him. He'd sensed a sly demeanour and a look of rat cunning about one of the new men as they'd sailed up the river. And the first mate had told him that it had been Dirk, who had been overseeing the rigging that had fouled.

Untrustworthy and slack.

If he'd had the time before their hurried departure, he would probably have put him off the vessel. Sébastien's instincts when it came to a trustworthy man—or woman—had never let him down in all his years at sea.

He groaned. There were also the African slaves to consider. He could not let a gentlewoman wander at will on his vessel.

He dropped to the bed and leaned forward with his head in his hands. Taking over a slave trader's vessel would be fraught with danger and his ship was no place to have a woman.

Unbidden, Lisette's face filled his mind, and he tried to push it away. He needed no more pressure on his decision making. If she had heeded her father's wishes and not followed him to the quay on San Domingo, she would still be alive. Perhaps they had been too young, and that had contributed to the poor decisions he had made, but nevertheless, she was gone.

And I will not have the death of another young woman on my conscience. Another young woman who has been spoiled and is used to getting her own way. It was clear she had given no thought to leaving her uncle and the mortal danger which could await her in a town such as New Orleans.

"Are you all right, Captain?" A tentative hand brushed against his forearm and was pulled back quickly as he turned his head toward her.

He stared at her. This young woman had fainted. She was lying on the bed of a man who she believed to be a cutthroat pirate—he'd heard the stories—and the said pirate was sitting beside her in a state of undress.

And she asks me in that soft gentle voice if I am all right?

Sebastian pushed himself to his feet and pulled on his shirt. He turned to her. She lay on his bed and a little colour had returned to her cheeks. A dark green gaze held his and her eyes were wide. She opened her lips and a shaft of desire shot straight to his groin when the tip of her tongue came out and touched on her bottom lip.

"Are you thirsty?" He knew his voice was gruff because he was angry at the reaction of his body to this helpless female.

But perhaps not so helpless. Is she manipulating me?

She shook her head and tried to sit up but fell back onto the pillow with her hand to her head. "The room is moving."

"Yes." He stared at her. "The cabin is moving but I suspect it has more to do with us being in the ocean swell, rather than the faint you had. And I expect it will get worse as the day progresses. The wind is rising.

"Can you...can you...?

Before she finished she pushed herself up on her hands and slid back to the feather pillows and leaned back against the headboard of the bed. "Can you please take me back to New Orleans?" Her voice strengthened as she held his gaze. "I will make it worth your while."

Sébastien quirked an eyebrow. "And how will you do that, Madame? From what I see, you have the clothes you are wearing and a pair of slippers. Unless you have a bag of gold secreted in the alcove over there?"

"If you will turn your boat around and take me back, I shall be able to pay you when I...when I... in a few days." She set her chin straight and crossed her arms across the front of that hideous black dress.

"Why are you in mourning?" He ignored her request and the rather strange statement of being able to repay him in a few days. Perhaps she intended to sell her body in the taverns of New Orleans?

Over my dead body. Innocent eyes held his, and he was interested to hear what a young woman of breeding, in a mourning dress, was doing in a place as dangerous as New Orleans.

He stared down at her, keeping his face free from expression. "Shall we start at the beginning?"

Her pure beauty struck him afresh as she gazed back at him. Her perfect small white teeth worried at her lower lip and her emerald-green eyes were wide. Her heart-shaped face was surrounded by waves of auburn hair which rippled down her shoulders, falling almost to her waist. But her expression was steadfast and full of determination, and she held his eye unwaveringly. This young woman appeared to have a will of steel and he wondered what she was doing here.

I do not want her to be here.

She took a deep breath. "I cannot tell you everything because I do not know you well enough."

And she cannot trust me. Sébastien heard the unspoken intimation. She dropped her gaze for a moment before lifting her head and holding his eyes with hers again. "By all accounts, you sir, are a pirate and it would not be wise to tell you of my financial situation. It may put me at risk and I may not live to finish my quest."

Her quest? A strange term for a young woman to use. Sébastien dropped onto the bed and braced himself with his palms flat on the coverlet on either side of her. "So Madame, may I assume you have been in the less savory establishments of New Orleans? Where else would you hear such scurrilous gossip about me?"

The girl straightened, and the bodice of her black dress strained over her high breasts. He dropped his gaze. For a young woman, she was well endowed but still she seemed unaware of her sensuality.

"Nay, sir. I have not set foot in establishments of any sort." The colour ran into her cheeks and he realised he was still staring at her chest, and that she was well aware of the direction of his gaze.

Sébastien cleared his throat and looked away to the wall above her head. He feigned a yawn to show his disinterest in her physical attributes. "Then perhaps you could begin by telling me your name and why you felt the need to hide yourself in my cabin. It appears to have been a matter of some urgency?"

She folded her arms and he avoided looking down at her breasts. "I was not hiding in your cabin. I was running away from my Uncle Titus."

"Why? Was he cruel to you?" Or God forbid, worse than that.

She shook her head. "No. Not by his hand, but I do not agree with his actions over the past six months, so you could perhaps call that cruelty."

Sébastien stood and walked to the side of the cabin to lean on the side of the hull, his hands laced behind his back and his head bowed. Her words echoed those of Lisette ten years ago.

Lisette had bowed her pretty blond head while she had told him of the cruelty of her father in not bowing to her will when he refused to approve their marriage. He would not let her have her own way and she too had rebelled. But her father had been right and if they had not been so young and foolish, they would have heeded his words, and Lisette would still be alive.

Perhaps they may have married, perhaps not. They had been far too young to make a decision about their future. Lisette had been naïve, and he had been a cocky and randy young man. A pretty face and a soft body had tempted him, and she had died because of him.

Sébastien didn't think of Lisette often now and that realization brought a rush of fresh guilt to his chest. He had loved her in his own way, but it had been an immature love which would surely have blown itself out like a storm at sea. He now had the opportunity to assuage that guilt. This young woman, who looked across at him, her eyes beseeching him, would be kept safe from harm by the lessons Sébastien had learned in the past.

"So, Madame, can you at least tell me your name?"

"I am Madeleine Bellerose of Bellerose Hall in Derbyshire in England."

Yes, wealthy and spoiled, just like Lisette.

"And why are you travelling with your uncle on a ramshackle old British frigate?"

Madeleine relaxed her shoulders and let

out a soft sigh. "My uncle is a member of some anti-slavery or missionary society, or some such, and we are travelling to the West Indies. We had free passage because he took the position of chaplain on the frigate."

"Yet, I am none the wiser as to why you are with him?" Sébastien's resolve was firming. Even if he had witnessed her uncle beating the young cabin boy, it was understandable. This young woman had been in the man's care and he thought he had lost her. Sébastien could fully understand and sympathized with the man's predicament.

"My family was killed in a carriage accident. My father, my mother, and my only brother are gone. Uncle Titus took over the family estate and dismissed the staff and made me accompany him to the West Indies."

"I cannot see what is wrong with that and why you felt you must escape. Surely someone must take care of you?"

Madeleine slipped her bare feet over the side of the bed and stood straight, her hands placed on her hips, as if to emphasize her words. "Why? I am quite capable of taking care of myself and running the family estate. You think because I am a woman, I cannot do that?" Twin spots of colour rose on her cheeks and her voice rose higher. "And he has had the temerity

to organize a marriage for me! I had to escape."
She sniffed and wiped the back of her hand
over her nose and Sébastien smothered a grin.
A mannerism he would not have expected from
a lady, more from a young child. Sympathy
tugged at him and he pushed it away. Her
presence on his vessel was problematic for him
and he would not be taken in by her feminine
wiles.

"If Uncle Titus wanted to travel to some
godforsaken part of the world and minister to
heathens and save slaves, he did not have to
drag me along. I am more than capable of
looking after myself."

Sébastien's interest was piqued. Save
slaves?

He wondered where they had been heading
and whether they were aware of the dangers of
such a pastime. It was time to teach this young
woman that she was too young to know it
all…and she was a woman, which to his way of
thinking automatically rendered her less
capable than a man in most pursuits.

Casually, he sauntered over to her and
stood so close that she had to tip her head back
to see his face. As she had told him, she
believed she was capable, and she showed him
no fear as she held his gaze steadily. However,
on closer scrutiny, the colour in her cheeks

deepened and her bottom lip quivered slightly as she waited for him to speak.

"Hmm." Sébastien reached out to her and clasped his hands together around her tiny waist. Perhaps she was laced into that dress; maybe that had contributed to her faint?

"So you are able to look after yourself? You are so capable you have no fear of coming aboard a pirate's vessel and being alone in the cabin of a notorious pirate such as I?" Sébastien lowered his face to hers until he could feel the warmth of her quick breath fanning his lips. It was time for her to see what foolish behaviour could lead to. She needed to be taught a lesson and he was prepared to take her in hand.

"You have caused me quite a significant problem, and I must think of a way for you to repay me. Without going back to New Orleans so you could do whatever it was you had planned. Whatever your quest was."

A rustle of stiff fabric preceded the warmth of her body pressing into his and he lifted his head slightly, surprised by her acquiescence. She pushed her body against his and lifted her hands to his chest. Perhaps he was mistaken?

Perhaps she is not the innocent I had taken her for?

As he gazed down at her, his fingers on her

slight shoulders, holding her close to him, her soft breasts pushed against his chest and a lazy swirl of desire kicked into his groin. Slowly he lowered his head and spread his hands across her back to hold her even closer. Her breath quickened, and her emerald eyes widened as her lips opened beneath his. He dipped his head down slowly, intending to briefly taste the sweetness promised by them. Just one lesson to begin with; he would not frighten her too much.

He felt her soft lips move to a smile beneath his in the second before her teeth fastened onto his bottom lip. She bit his lip with her pretty little teeth and pulled away from his hold.

Then a loud shriek escaped her lips as she stamped on his bare foot. "Take that, you…you, pirate! And don't you ever put your hands on me again, or I'll…or I'll…"

"Or you'll what, you little hoyden?"

Sébastien shoved her away none too gently, and she fell back onto the bed as he crossed the room to the pitcher of water, his hand pressed against his bleeding mouth.

***

Madeleine's heart was beating so fast, for a moment she thought she would faint again. She lay back on the bed and watched with a small measure of satisfaction as the pirate dabbed at his lip with a piece of damp cloth and she tried to calm herself. If he thought she was his for the taking, he was in for quite a surprise. Her breath was still coming in quick pants and she closed her mouth to focus on her breathing, waiting for him to come back over to the bed. She would fight him to the death.

What would he do? Dreading his touch, but in a strange way anticipating the feel of his hands on her again.

What is going to happen to me? She'd been brave enough when she had been sure of her ability to find her way through the streets of New Orleans and avoid being found by her uncle but now, she was in a much worse position than trying to find some lodgings in a strange town. She'd hoped to remain anonymous before she went looking for Aunt Josephine's house. Now, not only was she a captive, if the pirate was speaking the truth, they were out in the ocean and the vessel was leaving New Orleans farther behind with each wave it ploughed through.

Madeleine rolled over and pushed herself to her feet before he could touch her again. She regarded him steadily as he walked toward her.

He returned her gaze, but strangely Madeleine felt no fear. For all his words and threats—and his actions—she sensed that he would not go through with them.

Unless I am being naive, and it is only wishful thinking. Perhaps it was self-preservation that had dispatched her fear? Crossing the cabin toward him, she spoke slowly and clearly to convey her calm.

"Tell me what you shall do with me." A memory of the horror stories that Jake had told her of pirates making their captives walk the plank or abandoning helpless souls on desert islands flitted though her thoughts.

The man she now knew as Sébastien Leclerc, the pirate, ran a hand through his hair. Madeleine was used to seeing men in powdered wigs with their hair rolled back from their foreheads. She examined him as he let out an exasperated sigh. His hair, as black as a raven's wing, was pulled back into a piece of leather and his skin was deeply tanned. His eyes were a dark brown and ringed by long, dark lashes. She looked at the loose, white shirt which was still unbuttoned to his waist, and allowed her a glimpse of smooth skin on his chest which was as tanned as his face and neck. Her gaze dropped lower and still he didn't speak. A dark pair of close-fitting trousers moulded the muscles of his long legs and a rush of warmth filled her belly as she lifted her eyes back to his face.

His expression turned to one of amusement as he noticed her close examination. The warmth that had coiled in her belly now ran up her neck and onto her cheeks, as the gentle quivers in her private parts reminded her of the unfamiliar feelings she had experienced when she had read Aunt Josephine's diary.

Oh no. She would not let these strange feelings take her mind off her quest. Madeleine put her hand to her mouth. Her desire to evade Uncle Titus and now the worry of being on a pirate's vessel and leaving New Orleans were uppermost in her mind, and would stay that way. She must figure out a way to get back to the New Orleans in order to find the heirloom and, more importantly, restore Bellerose for the friends she had left behind in England.

Frustration filled her and she dropped her chin to her chest. Determined she may be, but how she would achieve that was now out of her hands.

And in the hands of a pirate.

"You are quite the innocent, aren't you, Madeleine Bellerose?" He reached out and took her hand, his clasp strong and warm, yet still she felt no fear.

"Please?"

"Please what? Tell me how I may please you? Is that what you ask?" His deep voice washed over her, and she closed her eyes.

"What will you do with me?"

She lifted her head again and brushed the back of her hand impatiently at the tears that spilled onto her cheeks. She met his hooded gaze. She would not appear as a lily-livered sissy. Father had always taught her to face adversity head on, and she allowed herself a grim smile. One thing she was certain of, when Father had been teaching her that, he would never, in his wildest dreams, have imagined her being orphaned, on the other side of the world and a captive on a pirate ship. But the lessons he had taught her had made her the person she was.

The pirate lifted his hand and wiped away the tear with the pad of his thumb and his kindness opened a flood of tears. Madeleine sank to her knees and put her hands over her face as she gave into loud sobs that wracked her body.

"Come now." His voice was kind as he lifted her to her feet and led her back to the bed, but Madeleine couldn't stem the flow of tears. "I promise I won't hurt you. You are quite safe with me."

"I am not frightened." She hiccupped. "I just don't know what to do."

"Well, then, compose yourself and we

shall decide what is going to happen." The bed dipped beneath his weight as he sat next to her. "I can certainly tell you what to do."

She strained to hear as he muttered beneath his breath. "I should turn the vessel around now."

"What shall I call you?" The sobs had subsided, and she sniffed, again using the back of her hand in a most unladylike manner.

"You can call me Sébastien. That is my name."

"Where are you from?" Finally, she could speak without crying. Madeleine straightened her shoulders and looked to the man sitting beside her. "Where is your home?"

"Where am I from?" Smile lines formed around his eyes as his lips tipped upward in a wide smile and a warm watery feeling ran through her. "I am from many places. I consider no place on land more home than another. Why do you ask?"

Madeleine sensed he was trying to calm her with conversation. "Your words? Your accent? You speak like no one I have ever met before."

"I was born on an island called San Domingo, but for the present my home is on this vessel." He held her gaze and that funny feeling crawled back into her belly. It was not unpleasant, and she filed it away to examine later.

"My mother was the daughter of a French settler…and my father? Well that's another story for a time when we are bunkered down in a storm. I consider myself neither French nor American."

Madeleine swallowed. "Are you really a…a pirate?"

Sébastien's white teeth flashed against his tanned skin as he laughed. "I need to explore this assumption a little further. I believe that you watched my vessel from yours as we moored at the quay?"

Madeleine nodded.

"And did you see a skull and cross bones flying on our mast? Were we wielding cutlasses?" His grin got wider and she knew he was enjoying teasing her. "Did you see the fair citizens of New Orleans running away in fear as they beseeched us not to murder them in their beds?"

This time she shook her head slowly and it was hard not to smile at the playful tone in his voice. She bit her lip.

"So tell me, why do you think I may be a pirate?"

"Jake…the cabin boy told me stories of Sébastien Leclerc who is a pirate feared across the oceans."

"Ah, did young Jake, indeed? Perhaps I will have to have a word with him." He tapped a long elegant finger against his cheek and Madeleine watched fascinated as his tongue ran around his top lip. Then she realised what he'd said.

"Jake? How can you have a word with him?"

"Young Jake has come on board the *Maiden* for our voyage and by the sound of things he may be as pleased to see you as you may be to see him."

Relief coursed through Madeleine as she realised she may have an ally on board, and then it was quickly dispelled by his next words.

"You shall see him in the morning. Now we must get some sleep, but until I am sure I can trust you to stay below deck in my cabin, you will share my bed."

Sébastien stood and reached behind Madeleine and pulled the coverlet down on the soft bed. She stifled a gasp as he shrugged his shirt from his shoulders and her vision was filled with a bare chest.

"Although if you do go above deck, there is nowhere for you to run to." He pointed to the far side of the bed that was tucked into the side of the hull. "I shall sleep on the outside and if you need to get out to use the privy—" the heat filling her already hot cheeks increased "—you will have to wake me. But rest assured the first attempt to escape my cabin and I shall be forced to tie your hands to the bed." His voice softened. "I do not want to go to those lengths, Madeleine, but trust me, I will. It is for your own safety. Now can you sleep in that ugly black dress or would you like to take it off?" The grin was back, and her face burned.

Madeleine turned her back and scurried over to the far side of the bed and pulled the coverlet over her chest and up to her chin as Sébastien walked over to the lamp. The muscles flexed in the smooth golden skin of his back as he reached across and snuffed the wick. The room was immediately immersed in pitch darkness as the sweet smell of oil permeated the small space and she held her breath as the bed moved beside her. Rolling over, she turned her face to the wall and presented her back to him. A low chuckle near her ear preceded the warm hand that settled on her hip and she closed her eyes waiting for what would surely follow. Madeleine had some idea of what to expect when she married, and she squeezed her eyes shut, preparing to be ravished.

But Sébastien's hand stayed there without moving and his soft voice filled the tense silence. "Now try to sleep and we shall talk more in the morning."

Madeleine lay beside him, her body rigid and her heart thudding against her rib cage. She tensed as the bed moved once more.

What was he going to do?

"Oh, and Madeleine. I'm not really a pirate, but I would appreciate it if you don't disillusion young Jake on the morrow." His laugh sent heat spiralling though her body and she squeezed her legs together to try to capture the exquisite feeling that consumed her as the pressure of his hand weighed through her dress onto her skin.

"I think young Jake is quite chuffed to think he is a cabin boy on a pirate vessel."

The bed creaked as he lifted his hand and turned his back to her. Soon only his soft steady breathing could be heard over the creaks and groans of the boat as it pushed through the waves, taking her farther from her destination with each gust of wind in the sails.

She would not give in to sleep. Another escape must be planned, but Madeleine suspected that the man lying next to her was going to be much harder to hoodwink than Uncle Titus.

Chapter Eight

Madeleine dreamed of emeralds and diamonds, and Aunt Josephine who was repeating the words which Madeleine had imprinted in her memory. Aunt Josephine was walking beside a row of graves and Madeleine shivered in her sleep.

What new passions will my lover find me today? What pleasures unheard of, undreamed of? A wavering old voice said the words she had read in the diary.

Madeleine woke slowly, reached up and stretched before she opened her eyes. She frowned and twisted in the bed; the long skirts of her stiff, black dress were caught around her knees. She reached down to untangle herself. A gasp escaped her and her eyes flew open when her hands were captured and held above her head. In her dream, she had been safely in the garden at Bellerose, and then in a cemetery looking for Great Aunt Josephine, but when she opened her eyes, she encountered a pair of dark brown eyes examining her closely and the events of the last day came rushing back to her.

"Good morning, Madeleine." Sébastien's voice was husky with the remnants of sleep but his eyes were alert and full of interest as he scrutinized her. "I need to go above deck very soon but first we shall set some rules for you."

He set her hands free, rolled to the side of the bed and stood, all in one quick fluid movement.

A good thing for me to take note of. His eyes were keen and he moved quickly. Not that there was anywhere for her to run to while she was on the boat, but she filed that quick, feline movement away for future reference.

"Stay there." He disappeared behind the curtain beside the door and Madeleine sat up to take stock of her surroundings. During the night she had been too focused on finding a hiding place to notice the cabin and then when she had been discovered, her attention had switched to preserving her safety.

And what a cabin it was. He said he was not a pirate, but Madeleine was sure that the captain's cabin on the frigate on which she had spent the past month would not boast a cabin as luxurious as that which she was observing. She had not seen what a huge space it was; it must run half the length of the vessel. She turned her head and her gaze followed the solid timber beams which lined the base of the deck above her. The dark beams were richly oiled, and the bedclothes and the curtain were ruby red and shot with gold thread. A second table she hadn't noticed last night held a bowl filled with some sort of purple exotic fruit which she did not recognise. Eventually curiosity and hunger got the better of her. She climbed from the bed and her bare feet encountered a deep, soft carpet. It was richly patterned and of the same deep red as the curtain across the room. Shaking her head, she allowed her gaze to wander over the furnishings. The contents of this cabin were more suited to a Duke's drawing room and were far more elegant than anything that had filled Bellerose Hall even before Uncle Titus had sold most of it. If Sébastien Leclerc was not a pirate, as he said, he appeared to be a very rich sea captain. She padded quietly over to the table, lifted the unfamiliar fruit and turned it around before sniffing it.

"Are you hungry?" The deep voice came from close behind her and she twirled around. Sébastien stood beside her. He was as sure-footed as a cat in the dark. She had not heard him approach.

She nodded as her stomach emitted a loud grumble and heat flared in her cheeks. He gestured to the curtained area. "Perhaps you may care to…er…freshen up? You will also find a table with a pitcher of water and a bowl in there."

Madeleine walked past him, keeping her head high, but she was aware of his eyes on her as she pulled the curtain down behind her.

***

Sebastian had feigned sleep in the early hours until he had been sure that Madeleine Bellerose had fallen asleep herself. He had lain there in the dark, until her soft breathing had fallen into a regular pattern and her body had relaxed against his. For an hour he had lain there, his mind ticking over, and it had been almost light before he'd allowed himself to drift into a light sleep. Now he sat at the table, waiting for her to come out from the privy. He had formulated a plan before dawn and she must agree to it. He suspected, however, that she may be reluctant to fall in with his idea. If she wanted the freedom of the vessel while they were out at sea—when they were at Barataria Bay, it would be a different matter— she was going to have to listen to him and agree to what he proposed.

She will have no choice but to agree—for her own safety.

Madeleine stepped from the privy and

dropped the curtain and walked slowly over to him. Again he was struck anew by her innocent beauty—a virginal beauty, he was sure. Her face was still rosy from sleep and her long auburn hair was loose and hung over her shoulders hiding the neckline of the ugly, black dress. Her hair was thick and of the richest auburn he had ever seen. He stared at her for a moment longer before pointing to the chair opposite him. The contrast between her alabaster skin, the deep green eyes and her auburn tresses was breathtaking, and he found himself almost bewitched. If she was any other woman—apart from an innocent virgin—he would have had a most pleasurable time with her in his bed during the voyage.

But it was not to be. He hoped it would not be difficult to convince the crew that she was his woman—so long as she would agree to go along with his plan. It was the only way to keep her safe; and that he must do. Only Mr. Abrahams would be aware of the truth of why she was onboard. But she could not appear on deck in a mourning dress if they were to convince the crew she was his wench. He hoped that she would not be recognised as the young woman who had laughed down at him when he had fallen from the rigging into the Mississippi River. But her bonnet had hidden her features and the two ships had been far enough apart so that the crew would not have seen her face. Once she was out of that ghastly black dress and left her hair down, she would not be recognised as that same young woman at all.

"I assume you are wearing the only clothes that you have here?"

She nodded, and her expression was wary. "Yes, the rest of my clothes were in my bag that Jake threw overboard."

"Jake? The cabin boy?" Sébastien frowned. He would have to bring young Jake down here before it was known that Madeleine was on board. But first things first; something had to be done about her attire.

"Do you have any seamstress skills, Madeleine?"

Before she could answer, there was a tap at the cabin door.

"Yes, who is it?" Sébastien followed it by a yawn so that whoever it was would think he was still abed.

"'T is Crawford, Captain. I have heated some porridge for the crew and brought some for you."

"Wait there. I will be with you in a moment." It was time to put his plan into place but it was a shame that he had had no time to tell Madeleine what she was going to do.

Sébastien put his finger to his lips as he stood and walked around to where she was sitting. Lowering his head, he lifted her hair away from a delicate shell-like ear, ignoring the jolt of warmth that ran up his arm as her hair brushed his skin.

"You are going to have to trust me. All right?" he whispered as he grasped her arm and pulled her across to the bed, before he gestured for her to climb back in.

Sébastien reached across to her dress and tried to look apologetic as he took the fabric on her shoulders between both hands and ripped it, exposing her bare skin. He tucked the loose fabric down, so it barely covered the soft swell at the top of her breasts.

"Now lie back, muss your hair and try to look wanton."

"Wanton?" At least she kept her angry response to a whisper. "How do I look wanton, pray, captain?"

"Pinch your cheeks and bite your lips to redden them." He lifted his fingers to his bruised lip where she had bitten him. "You need to look as though you have been tumbled in my bed all night. Now get that sour look off your face and smile."

Comprehension dawned in her expression,

and she did not need to pinch her cheeks as the colour flooded into them.

A virgin. He would put a wager on that assumption.

Sébastien was pleased to see Madeleine follow his instructions as she lifted her fingers and ran them through her thick, loose tresses. As he walked slowly across to the door, he unlaced his shirt and pulled it from his breeches.

Grasping the wooden door handle, he stood to the side and opened the door, allowing the ship's cook to enter and place the wooden tray he was carrying onto the table they had just vacated.

"Thank you, Crawford." He feigned another yawn and gestured to the bed. "I had not realised it was so late in the morning. I am surely a layabout today. I have had little sleep." He winked at the man and inclined his head to the bed. "Please tell Mr. Abrahams I will be on deck shortly. If Madame lets me leave."

Crawford glanced across to the bed and his grin exposed the gaps that missing teeth had once filled. "Aye, aye Captain." His gaze lingered a little too long on Madeleine's chest for Sébastien's liking and the protective instinct that rushed through him brought back thoughts of Lisette. He stepped between the man and the bed to block his view, and pointed to the door. The cook had seen enough for the assumption to be made.

"Thank you, Crawford."

The door closed behind him and Sébastien put his finger to his lips as he held Madeleine's gaze. When the sound of the cook's footsteps had receded, Madeleine jumped from the bed, clutching her torn dress to her chest.

"My question was timely." Sébastien leaned against the door and watched as Madeleine's chest rose and fell as she tried to contain her anger.

"What question?" She glared at him and he stifled a smile. He didn't need her angry; she must be receptive to his plan, which thanks to the cook's timely visit, would be well under way by now. The presence of a woman in the captain's bed would be spread round the crew like wildfire.

"About whether you have any seamstress skills?"

She walked across to the table and sat on the chair, still clutching her torn dress together in front of her breasts. "So, you intended to tear my dress all along?"

She has courage.

"No, that was necessary in the circumstances; however, we do need to find you some suitable clothes."

"What do you mean suitable?"

Sébastien crossed the room and crouched beside her. "By now, the word will be spreading above deck. The captain has a luscious wench below and the crew will be salivating to see what manner of woman has caught the captain's eye this—" He broke off before he could finish. Madeleine narrowed her eyes.

"This what?"

"Nothing." She did not need to know that occasionally a woman would accompany him on his voyage. Although it had been a few months since he had given passage to the dark-haired beauty who had needed a berth from Antigua to New Orleans. The fact that she had ended up in his cabin was of no concern now; of prime importance was keeping Madeleine safe from harm. He had never taken a woman on any of the governor's missions; that would have been foolhardy. He had yet to give thought as to what he would do with Madeleine when the mission was over, and they returned to New Orleans. That was in the future and if her uncle was still in port—which he doubted—Sébastien would hand her over.

"Yes, I can sew." Her quiet voice interrupted his musing.

"Good." Sébastien took her hands in his and examined them. There was no doubt she was a gentlewoman. Her hands were soft and white, and he held them gently as he lifted his gaze. Her green eyes were fixed on his and a pulse fluttered in her slender, white neck.

"Being a lady, I would not expect you to have much knowledge of life aboard a vessel?"

She shook her head. "I have knowledge. Do not forget, Captain, I have just travelled across the ocean from my home."

"On a British frigate with a chaplain on board? A very different proposition to a pirate vessel, my dear."

A gasp escaped her lips and she pulled her hands from his grasp. "You lied. You said you were not a pirate."

"I'm not…exactly. But there will be some…shall we say…action while we are at sea. That is why it is imperative that you must listen to me and do everything I say."

He lifted his hand and trailed his fingers down the side of her soft cheek and her eyes widened.

"Everything," he repeated softly.

Chapter Nine

Everything.

Madeleine took a deep breath as the blood drained from her face, and her ears began to buzz as the word brought her fear clawing to the surface.

I will not faint again.

She swallowed and held the gaze of the man who was crouched in front of her. His shirt was still open, and he was so close she could see the fine hair covering the golden skin of his chest. Never before had she seen a man at such close quarters, especially one whose warmth was tempting her to lean closer and place her hands against his skin. She clenched her fingers together, resisting the strange temptation.

To lay my open palms on his chest and rest my head on his shoulder would be…would be…safe.

Confusion swirled through her. Rational thought told Madeleine she should be very frightened, but she was not. Just a little exciting trickle of fear that sent goose bumps running down her arms. Waiting for him to explain what "everything" meant filled her with a dangerous sense of anticipation.

"It is most important that the crew believes you are my woman." He lifted his hand and touched the stiff fabric of her dress. "What are you wearing beneath that?"

The heat began where his finger had brushed her shoulder and continued up to her neck. Robert, her dear brother, had taken great delight in tormenting her about her propensity to blush and she knew how much her fair skin betrayed her feelings.

"A chemise, a corset and a camisole." Madeleine took a deep breath and willed her face to cool.

"Good Lord, woman. No wonder you were in a tangle when you awoke." He grinned at her and now the warmth travelled down to her abdomen as well as up into her face. "But that is good. It will give you something to work with. I assume your undergarments are not black?"

She shook her head. Her undergarments were a pretty, lacy white and threaded with the colourful ribbons that Father had bought her from his visits to town. She had ensured that she had sewn them into her undergarments so there would be a constant reminder of her family, no matter what she encountered in this new, unknown world. Uncle Titus had frowned at any colour on her black mourning garb so her ribbons had remained well hidden from his view. Perhaps now they would be visible?

Sébastien stood and crossed to an ornate chest which rested against the end of the high bed. She waited while he lifted the lid and grunted with satisfaction. An article of clothing such as she had never seen before dangled from his fingers. It was a brilliant red with black ribbons lacing the front together. He handed the soft silken fabric to her, the grin still on his face.

"Now, I must go above deck. You will be busy." He gestured to the food on the table. "Eat, before you begin."

"Ah, Sébastien?" It was strange to say his name but that was what he had said she was to call him.

He stood and tucked his shirt into his breeches, before swiftly lacing up the ties and drawing the white fabric together over his chest. "Yes?" He glanced across at her.

"Before I begin what?"

"Begin to do something about your appearance. The black dress must go, and you can put an outfit together. Something that befits a pirate's woman. With that—" he pointed to the scrap of silk she held "— and your corset, you should be able to fashion something suitable." He strode to the door and looked back at her before he opened it. "But be quick about it, we must talk to Jake before he gives away who you are. Once I speak to Mr. Abrahams, my first mate, I shall bring Jake down here. We will have to let him into my plan to keep you safe. I shall be back down within the hour."

Madeleine sat at the table for a few minutes after the door closed behind him. She examined the flimsy piece of red silk that Sébastien had passed to her and pulled a face. It appeared to be a top garment of some sort that would go over a skirt.

Aware of the time passing, she dipped her finger into the porridge that had now congealed into a glutinous mess, tasted it and immediately spat it back into the bowl in a most unladylike manner. It was laden with salt and foul tasting; if this was the food on a pirate vessel she would not be partaking of any more. Reaching for the small purple fruit she had examined earlier, she took a tentative bite. An explosion of sweet juice filled her mouth and Madeleine closed her eyes; the soft flesh was as sweet as the spun sugar confections that Cook had made back home. She dropped her head into her hands and wondered what she was doing here on a pirate boat, about to transform her appearance to that of a pirate's wench.

I should have hidden from Uncle Titus in Derbyshire until he left me behind, and never set out on this foolhardy adventure.

Madeleine allowed herself to wallow in self-pity for only a moment before she shook her head, and brushed away the lone tear that rolled onto her cheek.

I am here and I will make the best of the circumstances I am in.

Raising her chin, she sought the determination that usually filled her. A maybe-pirate and a pirate ship would not deter her from her planned course. She would continue with her quest and seek out the emerald and diamond necklace and then travel back to England to triumphantly restore the family estate. And if that meant spending some time masquerading as the doxy of a man who may be a pirate—or not—so be it.

Madeleine stood and reached around to the back of her dress and began to unlace the ties holding it together at her waist.

***

The wind was blowing stiffly from the south and it carried the smell of a squall not far off. The sails snapped sharply as Sébastien crossed the deck to the wheelhouse and took over the steering. He listened as Mr. Abrahams informed him of their bearings before the first mate went below deck to break his fast. They were close to Grande Terre and about to enter the narrow channel separating the island from the reed marshes of the delta country where Jean-Luc had his trading outpost, and they would re-provision the vessel. They must be quick. There was no time to lose. Sébastien observed the crew at work as he steered the boat through the rising waves. There was a big blow coming and he hoped they would be berthed safely in the shelter of Barataria Bay before it caught them. He would stay on board to ensure Madeleine's safety and send only a small party to shore to get the provisions. He also had no desire to see his half-brother. He wanted Jean-Luc to have no inkling of his plans. Sébastien cast his gaze around the vessel as he decided who to send to shore.

The sail maker and his idler were repairing a torn sail which was spread across the top deck. Young Jake was sitting on a barrel watching them; the swelling on his eye had gone down a little, and shades of purple and blue were high on his cheek. Sébastien slowly scanned the decks above and below his vantage point as the strong wind filled the sails and the vessel picked up speed. The boatswain was supervising the Africans as they scrubbed the lower deck. Sébastien allowed himself a brief smile; they were more energetic than any of his crew when deck washing was underway. The three new crewmen were nowhere to be seen and he narrowed his eyes. At this time of the morning all crew should be above deck and working at one duty or another. There were always tasks to be done to keep the vessel in good order. He was a hard, but fair taskmaster, and his crew was well used to his ways. For a moment, he considered putting the three new men ashore at Barataria Bay. He could not afford to have a less than committed crew, but then he realised that they would need a full contingent for this mission and there was no time to rouse up new crewmen. They would soon learn the ways of his vessel.

"Bear into the wind, Mr. Abrahams." The first mate had come back up the ladder and had taken over the wheel from Sébastien. "There's a squall coming from behind. Grande Isle is three miles off." Sébastien pointed to the boiling clouds in the south.

"Aye, Captain."

They had made good time and would navigate the narrow channel between the two large islands into the bay before the weather broke. Sébastien turned to the first mate before he headed to the upper deck to speak to the cabin boy. "Where are the new crewmen? I will send them to shore to help with the provisions when we anchor in the bay."

Perhaps if he entrusted them with a measure of responsibility, they would feel more like part of the crew.

Mr. Abrahams gestured with a toss of his head toward the bowsprit. "All three are checking the stays of the foremast, sir. After the fouled rigging yesterday, I have set the crew to check every rope and every stay on the vessel." He grinned. "I don't think they are used to being so meticulous."

"Well, if they are to stay on the *Maiden* they will soon learn they must be." As he walked toward the upper deck, Sébastien glanced up to the rigging. All looked to be in order from below. "I am taking young Jake to my cabin to check on his eye."

The first mate threw him a curious glance but did not question him.

"Oh, and Mr. Abrahams." Sébastien allowed a slight smile to cross his face. "We have another passenger on board. There is a young woman in my cabin. I would not want you to be surprised when she comes on deck."

The man looked back at Sébastien with a frown. "Pardon, sir. Is that wise considering the nature of our voyage?"

"It could not be helped. I shall explain when there are no ears to listen." He gestured to a couple of the crew who were working close to the wheelhouse and Mr. Abrahams nodded.

"Later." Sébastien nodded and climbed the stairs to the upper deck. Young Jake jumped to his feet.

"Captain." He bowed his head respectfully and Sébastien ruffled his hair casually.

"How is your head today, boy?"

"Much improved, sir."

Sébastien was pleased. The boy had much potential and would do well if he applied himself to learning the ways of his vessel. It was a shame he would not be here to take the boy into his care and watch him develop. He had no doubt the young lad would make a good seaman.

He gestured for Jake to follow him to the ladder and stepped back and let the lad precede him. When they reached the bottom, he turned and took the boy's arm and Jake's eyes widened.

"Don't be scared, I have a surprise for you. But it is imperative that you can keep a secret." He lowered his voice and stared at the lad.

"Can you do that?"

The boy nodded his head up and down respectfully, his eyes still wide.

"Come then, follow me." Sébastien tapped on the door and waited for a moment before he turned the handle and pushed open the door to his cabin. He stood back and let Jake enter before him.

Madeleine's dress was in a pile on the end of the bed, but the room was empty and Sébastien's heart seemed to stall.

Surely she hasn't left the cabin? There were two smaller cabins adjacent to his—the first mate's and a small space used for sick and injured crew. The only other place she could be was in the crew's general quarters at the other end of the lower deck, but surely, she would not have gone there?

This young woman is going to cause me much grief on this voyage. I know it.

Walking across to the curtain dividing the privy from the cabin, he kept his voice low. "Madeleine? Are you in there."

The curtain lifted slowly and Sébastien slowly let out his breath as relief filled him. He waited for her to step out from behind the curtain. A slender white hand was the first of her to appear as the curtain rose inch by inch, and then his heart kicked up a beat as

Madeleine stepped from the alcove.

A sensual woman, her auburn curls cascading over smooth white shoulders stood before him. One stray curl brushed a hint of cleavage barely covered by the ribbons and lace on the top of her red silken chemise.

Sébastien's mouth dried.

Holy Mother of Christ. He would not allow Madeleine anywhere near the crew dressed like that.

"Damnation," he muttered as he remembered he had instructed her to look just like that. But she had done a much better job of creating an outfit than he had ever imagined she would. His gaze travelled from her bare neck down to her waist. The chemise he had found in the chest was cut low and his eyes dropped further down. She had done something with that ghastly black dress and it now covered most of her legs. The problem was the fabric that now covered her lower half clung to her and moulded more curves than he'd ever imagined she had.

Two white shapely calves held his attention for a moment, and he reluctantly lifted his head.

Closing his mouth, he managed a husky "Madeleine," at the same time that Jake recognised her.

"Miss Madeleine. What in heaven's name has he done to you?" The small boy pushed past him and took Madeleine's hand with both of his. "If he's hurt you, I'll…I'll—"

"It's all right, Jake. Seb—I mean the captain—is taking care of me."

Sébastien grabbed the boy's shoulders as he clung to Madeleine's fingers. "'Tis all good, Jake. Your loyalty is admirable." His instincts had been right. This boy was of good stock. "But you must help me keep Miss Madeleine safe. Can you do that? There is good reason for her to be dressed like this." His lips twitched, and he fought the smile that finally tugged at his mouth as he appreciated her skill in transforming herself into a pirate's wench. "You are certainly a skilled dressmaker, Madeleine."

Sébastien forced himself to look away as Madeleine bent down to the young lad and put her arms around his shoulders as she hugged him in welcome. From where he was standing, he looked down the front of her loose chemise, to the tops of her rounded, creamy breasts, and the blood rushed straight to his groin. With a muttered oath, he turned and strode across to the table, pulling out two chairs, angry at the reaction of his body. It was as though they were two children play-acting and had no idea of the danger that was ahead.

"Both of you sit here. Now." A feeling of doom set in his bones which did not bode well for the mission ahead. "I don't have time for this."

There was no way he would allow these two young and innocent passengers on his vessel to interfere with the success of his mission. His future depended on it being successful. If needs be, he would imprison them both down here for the entire voyage and they could put up with being below deck for as long as it took to follow the governor's instructions.

The burden of keeping Madeleine safe was not going to take away from the success of this, his final mission. That was his quandary.

***

Madeleine looked across at Sébastien and a shiver ran down her back as her gaze settled on his face. His expression was thunderous and the kind expression she had become used to had left his eyes dark and glittering. Two hard lines were etched on either side of his mouth. Forcing herself to look away from his strong, handsome face, she stepped over to the table and sat on the chair he indicated, and Jake was not far behind her. Turning her head, she studied Sébastien's profile. His dark eyes were framed by long lashes, and his tanned skin gave him a rakish look. She was tempted to run her fingers over his chin, to feel the roughness of his chin, to see if the danger he emanated was real.

But they sat there quietly, and it was almost as though they were two naughty children in the school room about to be chastised by the schoolmaster. Madeleine stifled a grin. She was well used to that. Father had allowed her to attend the village school and her determination, and her sense of justice, had seen her in trouble on more than one occasion. She lifted her chin and held Sébastien's steely gaze. She would not allow him to intimidate her. No one would tell her what to do. She had had enough of that from Uncle Titus. She would be independent and make her own decisions from this time on.

The cabin was quiet and only the loud drumming of his fingers on the wooden table broke the silence. He observed them for a long moment before he finally spoke. Despite his silence and his fierce expression, Madeleine did not look away.

"Not doing exactly what I say could result in your death." His voice was cold and hard. "Do you understand what I am saying?"

Madeleine wet her lips and noticed

Sébastien's eyes follow the movement of her tongue. Somehow being dressed in these clothes—if they could even be called clothes— bolstered her courage and an unfamiliar loose feeling ran through her limbs. It was as though the removal of her constraining corset and dress had freed her modesty as well.

"Well, Madame?" He stared her down and she lowered her gaze to look at him beneath her lids. "What say you?"

"Yes…Captain." She kept her voice firm and steady. It was not the time to call him by his name.

"Listen carefully to me and remember every word I say." He settled back in his chair and crossed his arms in front of his chest. "Every word. Burn that into your memory. Your lives may well depend on it."

Jake sat there unmoving as Sébastien turned to him. "Lad, as far as the crew will know, you have never seen this young woman before today. It is essential that they do not know she is the young woman they saw on the frigate yesterday. Understood?"

Madeleine watched as Sébastien's expression lightened and he smiled at the young boy. "I don't mind if you pretend to strike up a new friendship, but it is imperative that they think that Miss Madeleine is my woman and that I brought her on board from a tavern in New Orleans before we departed." He flicked a glance her way. "Otherwise, she will be fair game. My men are good men, but men of the sea have little regard for the rules of society. The journey ahead is fraught with danger—"

Madeleine could not help herself. "If we are to do as you say, surely, we must know about you and your ship, Captain Leclerc?" Her voice was firm, and she lifted her chin. "What is the purpose of this journey and why are we in such danger? Surely your crew knows, so we have a right to know as well?"

He stood up and looked down at her, placing his hands on his hips in a cocksure stance. Despite his arrogance, Madeleine would not give in. "How can we trust you not to harm us? Or even worse, to not sell us to a slave trader?" Holding herself still, she studied his profile.

"You are right, Madeleine. If I were to be trusted I would have been dead a long time ago." He laughed and there was no mirth in the sound. "I will enter into a deal with you. I will tell you where we are going and the purpose of our voyage...if you tell me where you were going to get the money to pay me for your freedom."

She stared at him without answering and he leaned over her, his warm breath grazing her cheek.

Closer than a man should be to an unmarried woman of good breeding.

"Will you tell me, Madeleine?" He straightened, and the warmth of his thigh pressed against her shoulder almost burned her skin. A strange feeling ran through her nipples and a shaft of something sliced through her as a throbbing heat settled between her thighs. It was as though they were alone in the cabin and she swallowed as a reckless urge to press herself against him consumed her.

Swiftly, the heat ran into her neck and face and she stumbled over her words. "I…I will…I may consider it."

"And so may I," he replied. "Now we are about to anchor in Barataria Bay and stock the boat with food and water for the voyage ahead of us." Sébastien crossed to the door. "Come with me, Jake."

Madeleine smiled at the lad as he shot a sympathetic glance her way.

"Madeleine, once the boat is steady at anchor, I shall take you above deck for a short stroll and my crew will see I have a woman on board. A brief visit only, as bad weather is about to come in from the Gulf, and it will not be pleasant even though we are leeward of the Grande Isle."

Madeleine inclined her head gracefully and feigned disinterest, even though she was keen to go above deck into the fresh sea air. But for the time being, she would do as Sébastien requested. He had frightened her with his talk of death and his wild crew.

Is he a pirate? Is that why he is so suddenly interested in my purpose in New Orleans? She would guard that secret closely and would speak to Jake at the first opportunity. She must ensure that Jake did not share the little information she had told him.

With no one. Neither Sébastien nor any of the crew.

Closing her eyes, she ran her hands down her dress. Strange and new feelings were coursing through her and she must not let that distract her from her quest. She had to trust that Sébastien would bring her safely back to New Orleans whenever his mission, or whatever he had to do, was done. How much to tell of her quest was something she was yet to decide. She could not risk that he would try to find Uncle Titus and return her to his care. She had managed to escape the clutches of one man who was determined to deny her independence and through unfortunate chance she now found herself in an identical situation with another man.

She stifled a groan. But now she had two secrets; the first was her quest to find Aunt Josephine's necklace. The second secret she would also hold close to her breast. Sébastien would never know of the feelings that rioted through her traitorous body every time he stepped close to her. Pirate or not, she had never before experienced the pleasant sensations that invaded her whenever he was in her presence and she would fight to the death to hide them. She could not allow him any more power over her than he already held.

Chapter Ten

Sébastien watched as the small boat reached the shore and the crew pulled it up above the tide line on the white sand in the distance. He'd included a message for Jean-Luc but was not sure that his half-brother would be at the outpost. He'd also had a quiet word to Mr. Abrahams about Madeleine and the grizzled old mariner had shaken his head.

"I hope you have not made a mistake in continuing with this voyage, Sébastien." The first mate knew this was the last mission on the governor's orders and it was already agreed that he would take over the captaincy of the vessel when Sébastien moved on. He was privy to Sébastien's plans to begin his own sugar plantation in the Hawaiian Islands, far from the seafaring world. Sébastien had shared with him the letter of marque from the governor authorizing him to free the slaves carried on the Ann Marie. How they went about it, and whether they removed any booty from the British trader was at his discretion. Jean-Luc would expect him to take the cargo, for distribution at his trading outpost, but Sébastien had little interest in that. His goal was purely to stop the Ann Marie from reaching port with the cargo of slaves. When that was achieved, he would receive his final payment from the Spanish governor and he could leave this life behind him. He had already formulated a plan for setting the slave trader Ann Marie on its voyage back to Africa and if all went to plan, there would be no bloodshed. Having the fifteen slaves on board his own boat already was fortuitous; he would broach his plan to their leader before they intercepted the Ann-Marie.

Now as he crossed to the ladder, his heart beat a little faster. He would watch Madeleine like a hawk when she was above deck. A reluctant smile tugged at his lips; she was certainly plucky. He had tried to frighten her into submission for her own safety but her demeanour and her reply that she would consider his deal, bespoke a brave and determined young woman. He knew she was still unsure of whether he was a pirate or a respectable captain and it would not hurt to keep her in doubt until their return. She might be more inclined to do as he said.

And as well as being brave and determined, she is also a very beautiful young woman. Now that she had shed the black mourning dress, her ripe beauty was far too tempting and Sébastien had to keep reminding himself of her innocence. He had already decided to take the night watch from Mr. Abrahams, so he didn't have to spend the nights in his cabin with Madeleine breathing softly beside him in the bed. He shook his head as he descended to the lower deck. It would be an utter waste if she ended up as a missionary's wife in some godforsaken settlement. She would be more at home in an elegant drawing room in a wealthy man's home. Greeting her guests with her bare white shoulders glowing softly in the candlelight, and her delightful auburn hair swept up and set with jewels.

A waste. He banished the thought as he opened the cabin door. Her future and where she may spend it had naught to do with him and he would leave off worrying about that until the *Maiden* was safely docked back in New Orleans.

Madeleine was still seated at the table, her fingers playing idly with some lengths of coloured ribbon. She glanced up at him and the light caught a sheen of tears in her eyes. She dropped her gaze and folded the ribbons and placed them on the table before lifting her head up.

Her eyes were clear and dry; the sheen must have been a trick of the light.

"Are you ready to come up on deck?"

Madeleine nodded, and he stood back to let her precede him. He frowned as she stood in front of him at the cabin door and smoothed her hands nervously down the front of her skirt. There was something lacking. Her arms were bare, and he hesitated before he reached past her for the door handle.

"Wait." Sébastien crossed to the small chest and lifted the lid. He pulled out a handful of the gold bangles that had been there since Jean-Luc had captained the *Maiden*. Sébastien had taken over the vessel to ply the river trade when his half-brother had decided to establish the trading outpost at Barataria Bay. Jean-Luc turned a blind eye to Sébastien's occasional foray to sea as long as there was some cargo retrieved for him. It was fair, they owned the ship jointly, and he'd be more than happy to hand the vessel over to Jean-Luc when he left. Sébastien would have no need of such a large vessel when he reached the Hawaiian Islands.

Moving closer to Madeleine, he reached out and took her arm, ignoring the nervous jolt that shuddered through him when his fingers brushed against her warm skin. "It would not look right if the captain's woman was not adorned with gold," he said quietly.

Madeleine stifled a soft gasp as he touched her arm but she held still when he pushed the small circlets of gold up over both of her wrists, along her forearms all the way to her upper arms. Her skin was the colour of alabaster and as soft as silk beneath his fingers.

"Yes, much better." He stood back and looked at her; the thought of her parading in those scanty garments in front of his crew made his stomach roil, but it must be done. "You are ready to do this?"

"I am." Her voice was soft and steady and, although her expression was calm, Sébastien's eyes were drawn to a pulse beating in her slender neck.

"It will be good to take a breath of fresh air," she said.

Sébastien let out a grim laugh. "And remember you will have to look at me not as though you wish to bite my lip, or stamp on my foot. You must look at me as though you are looking forward to pleasuring me tonight and reaping the rewards in more gold jewellery."

He took her arm and gave into a grin as her cheeks filled with colour and she glared up at him.

"You have until we climb the ladder to the deck to change your expression to one of lust and sensuality," he said.

"I will look the part but never in your wildest dreams should you think that I will be your strumpet." Her voice was cold but Sébastien was sure his dreams would be filled with her when he finally got some sleep.

***

Madeleine was conscious of Sébastien behind her as she climbed the ladder and his laughter followed as she hurried up ahead of him. Her soft shoe slipped on the last rung and she stumbled, landing in a most unstrumpet-like heap on the deck. He stepped out behind her and held out his hand and when he pulled her to her feet he held her close and dipped his head to whisper solicitously in her ear.

"Are you all right, my sweet?"

"Yes." Her anger had dissipated with the clumsy fall and Madeleine couldn't help the giggle that bubbled up from her chest. She looked down—at her very exposed chest. "Just my pride is bruised." Damping down her mirth, she switched her expression to the most adoring look she could muster and ran her fingers lightly down his jaw before pausing, and then brushing her fingers across his firm lips. His chin was as rough as she'd imagined, and she took a little satisfaction in the nervous tic pulsing his cheek as her fingers traced along his mouth.

The pirate did not speak again but held her close and looked down at her as her fingers played on his face. Warm shivers radiated from where his hands held her firm and close to his hard body. Madeleine held her breath; she had never realised that a man's muscles were so firm. Finally, he loosened his hold and stepped back. She took in a deep draught of salt-laden air. Her head was spinning, and the cool breeze was welcome on her overheated skin. Sébastien took her arm and walked her across to the bow, pointing out the features of the vessel as they slowly crossed the deck. She knew he was ostensibly bragging about his vessel to his woman and wanted it to be seen as such.

And it is a fine vessel. She had not taken much note of the *Maiden* when it had sailed past the frigate in the Mississippi, but now her wide–eyed admiration was not feigned. The oiled timber gleamed, and nothing was out of place on deck. Barrels were stacked neatly alongside the hull and tucked into the spaces between the decks. Ropes were coiled in neat, thick circles along the side of the hull. If it had not been so dark when she had come aboard, she may have found a hiding place on the deck and gotten off the vessel when she had seen it was going to leave. As they strolled along with her hand tucked into the crook of Sébastien's arm, the sun broke though the heavy cloud above and the wind eased back. The sun burned hot on the bare skin of Madeleine's shoulders and she looked around for some shade. A nervous flutter began in her stomach as Sébastien lifted his arm up to her shoulder and his fingers played on her bare skin. Everywhere she looked, they were being watched. Sailors were up the rigging, on the upper deck, and she felt her eyes widen as she noticed a group of men with the darkest skin she had ever seen. Sébastien's hand pressed into her back with a pleasant warmth.

"Come, I shall take you to the wheelhouse to meet Mr. Abrahams, my first mate. There is some shade there. Your delicate skin is burning." Madeleine froze as he dropped his head and pressed a kiss to her shoulder and a raucous ahoy sounded from the rigging above. She should have hated it but the warmth of his lips on her bare skin made her happier than she had been for many months.

As they moved to the centre of the lower deck, Sébastien called a friendly greeting to each crew member and gained a respectful reply. She looked up at him from beneath her lashes. He was a natural born leader and seemed to have the respect of his men. She just had to figure out what his leadership entailed. The vessel did not look as though it belonged to a pirate and his crew, and the men were certainly polite, yet she would heed his warning about the danger until she had made up her own mind and was more secure in her own safety.

"Ah. Young Jake." Sébastien paused and dropped his hand from Madeleine's shoulder. "This is Miss Madeleine, my…friend…from New Orleans. I would like you to keep her company when she comes up on deck in the day time, while I am occupied. It will be your main job, lad." He turned to Madeleine and spoke loudly for the benefit of anyone listening. "This is Jake's first voyage on the *Maiden*, my love, and he will be at your disposal."

My love. She knew it was a ruse but for a moment, she indulged in a wicked daydream that it was true before she stepped away from Sébastien's hold and smiled at Jake.

Jake dropped his chin and mumbled. "A pleasure to meet you, Miss Madeleine."

Madeleine inclined her head and smiled at him, but unease churned in her stomach. As soon as she was able to, she must tell Jake to hold her secret close. It appeared he too had fallen under Sébastien's spell. The man was too charismatic, and it did not bode well for the safety of her quest. Her opportunity followed immediately.

"Would you like to stay above deck for a while and take in some fresh air?" Sébastien gestured to a covered area behind the wheelhouse. "Jake, you can check that those ropes are clear of knots while Miss Madeleine sits with you and you may fetch anything she requires."

Jake's chest puffed with importance at the task he had been given and Madeleine watched from beneath her lashes as Sébastien took her arm once more and escorted her across to the shaded area on the lower deck. The heat travelling down her arm was from the hot sun. It was not from his warm fingers touching her bare skin.

It was not. She silently chastised herself for even noticing the pressure of his touch and tried to ignore the feeling that lingered even after he had lifted his hand away.

Sébastien nodded at her once she was settled on an upturned barrel and she reached down, tugging at her skirts, trying to cover her bare ankles with the short fabric, but to no avail. As he walked away she was sure there was an expression of mirth on his face. She watched as he walked across to where the dark-skinned men were folding sails at the front of the bow. He was taller than most of the crew and his stance was powerful. Broad shoulders and strong arms swung as he strode across the wooden deck. Her gaze dropped to the snug fitting breeches that moulded his long, muscular legs.

"So, what are you scheming, Miss Madeleine." Jake's lips were pursed in disapproval. "You are dressed as a doxy and on a pirate's boat and you are no closer to finding your hidden treasure."

"Ssh." She looked around with her fingers to her lips and hushed Jake, but they were alone. The closest crewman was a long way above them on the rigging. "I must beseech you to keep my secret. If this is indeed a pirate vessel, there must be no hint of me knowing of any treasure."

"What do you mean, if it is a pirate vessel? I told you about Sébastien Leclerc days ago…long before we even knew his ship would be in port, let alone that we would both end up on it. It may be a good thing for me, but certainly not for you." A frown crossed Jake's brow and he dropped his voice to a conspiratorial whisper. "As soon as the boat is provisioned we have at least two weeks' sailing ahead before we are back in port, and I know what is going to happen."

"How can you know?" Madeleine was concerned by the foreboding in Jake's voice. "And what is going to happen?"

"One of the sail makers told me. We are going to meet up with a ship called the Ann Marie and take her cargo."

Madeleine's blood ran cold. So it was true; because she had chosen this boat to hide on, her future was in the hands of Sébastien Leclerc, a pirate of the high seas. Why did he lie to her? So she would feel safe?

A man with no regard for honesty. What sort of position had she put herself in?

He must never, never, know about the heirloom. She would have no chance of returning to England and she would be lucky to leave his ship alive.

"Jake." She reached out and touched his arm and he looked at her earnestly. "You

must promise me you won't tell anybody about my aunt's necklace back in New Orleans. You must not tell. I cannot risk anyone else knowing about it. Can I trust you?"

"Of course you can." He smiled and held her gaze steadily before looking over her shoulder and jumping to his feet. "Look, the provision boat is returning. We will be underway soon."

Before she could stand and look to the

direction in which he was pointing over the water, Sébastien was walking toward them with his hand held out.

"Come, my dear." His voice was loud and carried across the deck. "We shall spend some time together below deck before we get underway." Heat ran up her neck as ribald laughter and comments drifted down from the sailors in the rigging once more. Madeleine held herself steady and regarded him. Despite knowing what he was, she could not reconcile the man in front of her with a black-hearted pirate.

Sébastien took her hand and pulled her to her feet. Jake averted his gaze as her chemise slipped even lower. She grabbed for it and a rude retort hovered on her lips; her intention must have been apparent to Sébastien. Before she could speak, his lips descended swiftly on hers and he murmured against her mouth.

"Keep calm. You have done well so far. But I want you below decks now."

She gazed up at him, as tingles ran through the nerve endings in her lips, but Sébastien raised his head and looked over her shoulder. "My dear brother is following the provision boat in his own flat boat and I would prefer he not see you when he comes aboard. He would insist on taking you to shore due to the…er…delicate nature of our voyage ahead."

For a moment, Madeleine considered perhaps going ashore would be in her best interests than heading out into the wide ocean with a buccaneer who was intent on purloining a cargo. "Could he get me back to New Orleans?"

Sébastien's gaze was hard. "My dear, one look at you in your current attire and you would not get out of his bedroom for a week. Then he would probably sell you to the highest bidder." He tugged at her arm. "Come quickly, his boat is almost upon us."

"And you won't sell me to the highest bidder?"

Sébastien grabbed her arm impatiently, led her around the wheelhouse and they remained out of view of the approaching boats as they climbed through the hatch to the ladder and below deck. He did not respond to her question.

As the cabin door closed behind them, Madeleine exhaled a heavy sigh and flopped onto the bed more like the way she was sure Sébastien would expect the cabin boy to act.

"You did well." He stood in the doorway and regarded her intently, but he did not smile and a shiver ran down her back. "Now I suggest you get some rest and stay quietly down here. I will come back and let you know when we are about to get underway. I hope you will not be seasick as it is going to be a very rough passage when we leave the Bay. There is a storm coming from the east." As if to reinforce his words, a gust of wind snapped the sails above as the squall approached.

Madeleine sat on the bed and watched as the door closed behind Sébastien. For the first time, she heard the slide of a bolt as he locked her in his cabin. Another shiver ran down her back and she rubbed her arms to quell the goose bumps that arose. For the first time since he had discovered her in his cabin, there was fear mixed in with the unbidden desire she felt for this pirate.

Chapter Eleven

Jean-Luc, Sébastien's less than honest half-brother, came across from the outpost on the provision boat and Sébastien was not pleased to see him. Jean-Luc turned as a sailor called down from the rigging and his eyes narrowed as he stared at the bow of the vessel where the Africans were sitting. His voice was as hard as steel and his eyes like flint as he turned back to Sébastien. "Slaves, brother? That is most unlike you. I thought you abhorred slavery or were they just pretty words to seek favour with your government friends?"

"Don't pretend to know me. I am aware that you have little care for what I do." Sébastien curled his fingers into fists and fought the desire to wipe the sneer from Jean-Luc's face with one well-placed punch. "Just be content with the work I do for you."

"Now, now, there is no need to feel under-valued. You are my brother, after all." He slapped Sébastien on the shoulder and

Sébastien's mouth dried as Jean-Luc turned to the hatch.

"You can surely share a brandy with me before you go? I am sure you have a fine bottle or two down in my old cabin."

Sébastien returned his half-brother's curious gaze and for a moment he wondered if Jean–Luc had seen Madeleine on deck, but he quickly dismissed that thought. There was no way he could have seen her and the new crewmen who had gone ashore were not aware she was onboard, so they would not have mentioned her presence on the *Maiden*. No, he was up to something and Sébastien wanted no part of it. As soon as they returned to New Orleans and he reported to Carondelet, he would leave the *Maiden* at the quay, and tell Mr. Abrahams to let Jean-Luc know he had gone. Then he would be on the first passage he could book to the Hawaiian Islands.

The sky darkened as a huge gust of wind buffeted the vessel and white horses began to whip up on the bay as the wind increased. The two boats were unloaded, and Jean-Luc's oarsman looked anxiously across the bay as a solid sheet of rain approached.

Sébastien held his half-brother's gaze and lowered his voice. "I am sure you are after something more than the pleasure of my company, so I suggest you tell me now or you will have to wait until my return."

And if all goes well, you will be waiting a very long time. Sébastien despised his half-brother and had kept his side of the river trade honest and free from corruption. That was more than could be said for Jean-Luc's dealings. If there was gold to be had, honesty was not a consideration he ever took into account.

Jean-Luc lifted his head and stared toward the squall that was coming in rapidly. "I won't ask where you are going, just ensure you are back in time to get the cargo delivered up river before the end of the month. There are many new river boats on the Mississippi and I would be most unhappy if we lost our market because you were off on some do-gooder mission. I know you too well, dear brother." He turned away with a laugh and then threw a final, casual question at Sébastien. "Oh, and by the way, were you acquainted with Ivan Lutchenko?"

Sébastien wrinkled his brow. At last, the reason for Jean-Luc's visit. "Lutchenko? The fur trader?"

"Yes." Jean-Luc grabbed for the side of the boat as it swayed in the rough waves. His oarsman gestured for him to jump into the smaller boat which was bobbing higher as the swell built. "I believe you took him upriver a few times?"

"I did. But that was more than five years ago." There was no harm in sharing that information with Jean-Luc. "Why do you ask?"

"There has been some talk of a missing family heirloom that he gave to his mistress and I wondered if you knew who his paramour was?"

Sébastien shook his head. "I barely spoke to him. He took passage on the boat once or twice when he was trapping upriver. From memory, he was a sad and taciturn man. I cannot imagine that he had anything valuable to give to anyone, nor that he had a mistress."

"No matter." Jean-Luc shrugged. "Have a safe…shall I say journey…or mission?" His laugh sent a shiver down Sébastien's back. "I will never understand you, my brother. You are a strange man."

Sébastien watched his half-brother climb down the ladder to the waiting boat.

And I will never understand the greed that drives you. With any luck, that would be the last time he would ever see Jean-Luc and the last conversation they would have. Sébastien turned away thoughtfully, as he prepared to issue instructions to lift anchor and drop the sails. The sooner the boat got underway, the better. The provisions had been stored and he would risk the squall. They would ride into the weather and leave it behind them as it headed toward the swampy bayous of the Mississippi delta.

He though fleetingly of Josephine du Bois and wondered if anyone else knew she had been Ivan's mistress. He let the thought go. It didn't matter. Josephine had died when her house had burned to the ground in the great fire of 1794. She had been laid to rest in the cemetery close to where her house had been in Rue Toulouse. If anyone was looking for her, they wouldn't have to look too hard. As for the heirloom, if there was one, it was long gone.

***

Madeleine lay on the bed in the cabin below deck as the timbers of the hull flexed and groaned. The wind roared, and the waves crashed against the bow as the storm continued. The vessel was pushing through a heavy sea and she had almost rolled from the bed several times. But she was not frightened. She was sure that Sébastien was an experienced mariner and his well-kept vessel was capable of staying afloat in these seas. As the roaring of the wind and the rocking of the boat lessened, she lay there and waited for him to come down to the cabin.

She knew she would have to share his bed, but she was strangely calm. Her eyelids were heavy, and Madeleine fought to stay awake, stifling a yawn as her head sank into the feather pillow. She had given much thought to his answer about where the vessel was going and had decided to ask more questions of him before she disclosed her reason for wanting to return to New Orleans. Finally, she could fight her tiredness no longer and she allowed her eyes to close.

Each time the ship came down hard on the back of a wave, she jerked awake before falling back into a light doze. Her dreams were filled with Sébastien and pirates with cutlasses, and an emerald necklace dangling just out of her reach on the mast. She rolled over and plumped out the feather pillow before settling back into a fitful sleep.

Hours passed and there was still no Sébastien. Dreams of home replaced her fragmented dreams of Sébastien and the boat.

When Madeleine came fully awake, it was pitch dark. The boat rocked from side to side, reminding her where she was. A sob caught in her chest—the dreams of home had been so real she had expected to wake up in her own bed at Bellerose Hall. Father would be so proud of her when she returned triumphantly with the necklace. She was sure he was watching down on her and he would know what she had done. Perhaps by now the Hall staff had managed to find work elsewhere. In one way, she hoped that they had, so they would not be hungry or without a roof over their heads. In another way, she yearned for everything to be the same when she came home with the necklace, and she could restore their positions. She reached out tentatively but the bed beside her was still empty.

For the first time since they had sailed from Bristol, doubt filled her thoughts and a cold feeling settled in the pit of her stomach. What if Uncle Titus had been right? Perhaps she should have listened to him and not been so determined that he was wrong. She sat up with a start and shook her head, sternly reprimanding herself.

I will not think that. I am right. Somehow, she would find the necklace and find her way home.

All would be well.

Slipping from the bed, she crossed to the narrow opening in the hull, and her stomach grumbled as she peered out. It was still dark outside; Madeleine shivered and rubbed her arms. The temperature had dropped and it was chilly standing on the wooden floor when she stepped off the square of carpet. A flash of lightning lit the cabin and a resounding boom in the far distance made her scurry back to the bed. She pulled the covers up to her bare shoulders; although it did sound as though the storm was easing and moving farther away.

Madeleine let a grim smile cross her face. She could face a wicked pirate any day and keep her wits about her, but a storm could bring her undone. The next boom of thunder was even farther away, and she prayed it would stop soon as she pulled the covers over her head. She had been alone for too long and her fears were finally taking over.

There was a slight noise at the door and she slowly lowered her hands and dropped the cover from over her face and waited, hoping it was Sébastien.

Tap. Tap.

She waited for a moment more and when the tap sounded for the third time she climbed off the bed and walked quietly over to the door, pressing her ear to the timber. It was quiet.

"Who…who's there?" The storm had shaken her, and she tried to keep her voice steady. She didn't know who would be knocking at the door, but she had to remember it was locked from the outside and not her side, and anyone who wished to enter could get in without much ado.

"Miss Madeleine, it's me, Jake."

Madeleine relaxed her shoulders and let out her breath. "What is it?"

"Cap'n sent me down to check you were all right." Jake sounded full of self-importance that he had been given a mission. "He said to tell you we have almost ridden the storm out and that Cook will bring you something to eat shortly."

"Thank you." Madeleine was surprised that Sébastien had even given her a passing thought as he had steered though the storm. "And Jake?"

"Yes?" His voice was muffled by a renewed groaning of the timber as the vessel rolled into a big wave.

"Thank the captain for his concern.

Chapter Twelve

Several hours passed before the ship's cook tapped at the door and slid open the bolt before passing in a tray with a bowl of broth and some biscuits. It must have been after midnight by that time, and Madeleine ate every morsel on the tray before climbing back into the bed and falling into a deep sleep.

Now, she opened her eyes and watched the shards of sunlight play across the timbered walls. The groaning and the rocking of the boat had eased, and it appeared to be slicing smoothly through the sea.

The storm had passed and Sébastien had not yet come back to the cabin. She was sure he would not have bunked in the crew's quarters as that would have appeared strange considering the crew knew he had a woman waiting in his own bed. Pushing back the covers, her bare feet touched the floor and she crossed to the narrow aperture in the hull. Blue sky and shining, flat silvery water filled her vision. After visiting the curtained area, and having a wash, Madeleine crossed back to the bed and sat looking around the cabin which was now lit with bright light through the apertures in the hull. She hadn't noticed there were so many. Even though she enjoyed her own company, this lonely confinement was unsettling her.

Throughout the next hour she moved from the bed to peer out through the narrow gaps, and then completed a circuit of the cabin. Eventually the small space became too confining and she crossed to the door. Sébastien had said that she had to follow his instructions to the letter, but surely, she could go above deck for some fresh air?

If she had to stay down here alone any longer, she would lose her sanity.

Madeleine stood beside the door and considered her options. At best, the Captain…the pirate…Sébastien would ignore her. She didn't even know what to call him in her mind. She could sit behind the wheelhouse again, take in some fresh air and have some of Jake's company. At worst, Sébastien would be furious at her for venturing out—she knew the door was unlocked because she had waited for the bolt to slide back when the cook had left but she had not heard it click in. She glanced over; the tray was still on the table where she had left it after finishing her meal.

Madeleine stared at the wooden handle and slowly reached her hand toward it, before snatching her hand back and folding her arms across her chest. It was cold down here; the sun would warm her, and if he asked she would explain that was why she had gone above deck.

Not because she was lonely… Why am I so intimidated by the man? It had nothing to do with being scared of him or the fact that he was a pirate, it had more to do with the fact that he had asked her to do as he said. She crossed back to the bed and sat, becoming more impatient as each long minute ticked over. There was no way she could stay down here for the whole voyage.

But did he tell me to stay here? The little voice of reason nagged at her conscience.

Not in so many words. He had said he would come back and see her when they were about to get underway.

But he didn't. So he had broken his word and she had not given her word that she would stay here. Not in so many words. She had promised to obey him. She had not promised to stay below deck.

Maybe Sébastien had forgotten she was down here?

But he did send Jake to check I was all right? And he did send the cook with food.

Madeleine stood and walked slowly to the door and stared at the handle again. She ignored it and pressed her ear to the door to listen. There was no sound to be heard; even the hull had stopped creaking. Tentatively, she reached her hand out and was about to touch the wooden handle when it lowered of its own accord and the door opened in front of her. She jumped back, letting out a small shriek at the sight of Sébastien filling the doorway. His black hair was dishevelled, and deep, dark shadows circled his eyes. For a moment, Madeleine was tempted to reach up and smooth the frown line that was between his brows, but instead she squeezed her hands together tightly in front of her chest.

"You were waiting for me to return? I hope you haven't been standing by the door all night?" The lines disappeared, and a smile tugged at his lips. Madeleine dropped her gaze from his, to stop the usual warmth flooding her.

But too late. A bronze-skinned, bare chest filled her vision. Her eyes remained fixed on that chest, slowly rising and falling with each breath that he took. The muscles across his broad chest rippled when he raised his hand to take her chin in his fingers. Madeleine's mouth dried, and she wet her lips.

"I…I was waiting." The words were slow to come. "I am tired of being cabin bound. I was worried for my sanity."

A low chuckle came up from his chest as his dark eyes held hers. "You may go above deck now while I rest. I have asked Jake to wait for you and keep you company. He has had some sleep through the night. Did the storm keep you awake?"

She nodded. "For a while. I have had some sleep, thank you." Why did she feel as though he was treating her like a child?

Almost telling me to go and play on the deck, like a good little girl. She lifted her chin, determined to have the last word. "And when you are rested, we shall discuss this voyage and my return to New Orleans, Captain."

His teeth flashed in his tanned face. "That we shall, Madeleine. Now run along like a good girl. Jake is waiting for you."

Madeleine tried to adjust her scanty clothing as best she could before she climbed the ladder, but it made little difference to the amount of her bare skin on display. She swallowed, climbed the final rungs and inhaled with pleasure as the fresh salt air brushed her face. She walked quickly across to the wheelhouse, nevertheless attempting to add a confident swagger to her gait. A couple of curious glances were thrown her way but most of the crew above deck were focused on their tasks.

Except for one. A stocky man with a red bandana tied around his head, a few greasy locks of hair plastered to his pock-marked neck leaned back against the rigging and stared down at her. She hadn't noticed him before. His mouth hung open in a salacious grin and his gaze dropped to her breasts. She raised her hands and crossed her arms, putting her head down and turning her back to the sailor when she reached Jake. He was sitting amidst a coil of ropes in the shade behind the wheelhouse.

"I didn't see that man yesterday." She jerked her head toward the man who was now working on the rigging. "He looked at me and it was awful."

Jake looked up. "He was one of the crew who went to shore for the provisions yesterday. Just ignore him." He nodded with wisdom beyond his years. "He probably hasn't seen a woman for a few months, and if you pardon me saying so, Miss Madeleine, you are a sight to behold."

"Thank you, Jake," she said with a wry note to her voice. "It is something I am not used to, that is for certain." She leaned back against the timber of the wheelhouse and let the warm morning sun soak into her bones. Despite sleeping after the storm had eased, weariness overcame her. She smiled at Jake when he dug in his pocket and pulled out a small bag. He removed a couple of biscuits the same as the cook had brought with her broth.

"Are you hungry?"

"Thank you." She grinned at him and took one. Not the sort of fare she was used to at home, but she was hungry, and they had eased her hunger last night.

They sat in silence for a while before Jake glanced around. "So, tell me more about this treasure you are seeking?"

Madeleine followed his gaze. There was no one within earshot and the rigging above them was empty. The horrid sailor with the bandana had disappeared.

"My Great Aunt Josephine sent me her diary. Well, in truth, she sent it to my father, but after he died I found it in his possessions." Madeleine held back a sob. "I never knew her. She lived in New Orleans and she apparently was the owner of a fabulous heirloom. A priceless emerald and diamond necklace."

Jake's eyes were as round as saucers. "And you know where to find it?"

"The diary gave me clues where to look." Madeleine hit her hand into her lap with a thump. "Now you know why it is so frustrating for me. If this pirate hadn't left the harbor like a thief in the night, I would have the necklace by now and I would be preparing for my voyage back to my home. The necklace will be enough to restore my family home to the way it was. And bring all the servants back."

Jake looked at her as though he was judging her. "I thought you were from a poor family and that is why you were with a poor ship's chaplain."

"I am a Bellerose of Bellerose Hall in Derbyshire and it is my task to bring it back to its former glory."

Jake spluttered. "With servants?"

She looked back at him and her voice was hesitant. "Yes, what is wrong with that?" No one had ever questioned her way of life before and she had taken it for granted.

"It is just as bad as the slavery over here."

"How is that so? Our servants are not oppressed like the slaves I heard Uncle Titus speak of. They are free to choose their own master and they are paid for their service."

"But they are still not free." Jake curled his lip.

"I know nothing of that." She drew herself up straight and her voice was as haughty as she could make it, and then she regretted it immediately. "I'm sorry Jake, let's not disagree."

"I'm sorry too. It's just that—"

"Just what?"

But Jake shook his head and changed the subject. "Why would your aunt have hidden the necklace? And how do you know it really exists?"

"In her diary she writes of a portrait where she is wearing the necklace." Madeleine closed her eyes and leaned back against the timber behind her back.

"And have you seen it?" He frowned.

"No, not yet, but I will find that, too." The sun was warm on Madeleine's face and she kept her eyes closed. "The necklace will be worth a fortune and when I sell it, I shall return home and Bellerose Hall will be filled with life and laughter again. All of my dear friends who worked there as I grew up will come back to work at the manor, and life will be as it was." A single tear spilled unbidden from the corner of her eye and ran hotly down her cheek. As nice as it would be, she knew it would never be the same without Mother, Father, and her brother Robert.

There was a stifled yell followed by a thud, and Madeleine's eyes flew open. At the same time a filthy hand landed on her chest, and pain shot through her as hard fingers squeezed her breast. She screamed and looked to Jake, but he was no longer sitting across from her. A pock-marked face filled her vision and she put a hand over her nose as the putrid breath of the man with the red bandana assailed her nostrils.

"Your little friend is over there, sweetheart." The sailor nodded to the other side of the vessel and she followed the direction of his gaze. Jake was lying in a crumpled heap against the side of the deck as though he'd been thrown there. There was no one else in sight; this man had chosen his time well to accost her. Madeleine opened her mouth to scream for help but his fleshy fingers filled her mouth and she gagged.

"Now keep yourself quiet." He looked around the deck with an evil grin and Madeleine's blood ran cold. "And tell me what you were about to tell your young friend. There is no one to help, so tell me what—" His breath left him in a soft oomph as Jake ran across the deck and head butted the sailor's flabby midsection. The man laughed and removed his hand from Madeleine's mouth long enough to pick Jake up as though he was a bothersome insect and throw him hard against the wall again. Madeleine opened her mouth and let out an ear-piercing scream as Jake hit the side of the wheelhouse and lay unmoving at her feet.

"Take your vile hands off me." She took a breath, but before she could scream again, the sailor moved his hand up to cover her mouth.

"Tell me where that diary is. No, we will make this quicker. Just tell me where I can find your treasure, and I will let your young friend live." His voice was a guttural whisper as his face pressed against her ear. With his other hand he reached down and grabbed Jake's hair. The young lad's eyes remained closed and a trickle of blood ran down his neck. Madeleine gasped around the fleshy fingers on her mouth as the glint of a knife flashed in the hand holding Jake's hair.

Before she could take it in, all hell broke loose. One of the dark-skinned men ran around the wheelhouse, scooped Jake from the deck up into his arms and moved away from the knife that the sailor was now brandishing from left to right.

"So, a heathen slave thinks he can best me, hey, matey?" The man's evil laugh turned Madeleine's blood cold. "Go back to your black brothers or I will kill the wench after I have my way with her."

There was a flash of golden movement behind him and suddenly Madeleine was freed from the sailor's deathly grip. She dropped to the deck, crawled to the wheelhouse and leaned against a keg with her knees pulled to her chin in an effort to stop her legs from trembling. Mr. Abrahams appeared beside the African man as Sébastien held the sailor firmly in a headlock.

"Pray that you live to tell the tale, you cur." Sébastien's deep voice sent a shiver through Madeleine and she looked up at him. He was shirtless and the powerful muscles in his chest and shoulders flexed as he held the man securely in his arms.

As she watched he turned the sailor around in one swift movement and pulled the man's hands up behind his back as the sailor let out a strangled yelp.

"Mr. Abrahams, see that this cur is locked securely in the hold for the remainder of the voyage." He looked to Madeleine as he spoke and she shivered at the hardness of his expression. He looked nothing like the man who had kissed her earlier.

When the sailors came running from the lower deck, he released the man into their hold. "You may walk the plank, yet, you dog. No man touches my woman and lives to tell the tale."

"No, Captain. No. Please no. I swear I didn't know she was your woman." The rough voice was now a snivelling plea, but to Madeleine's relief he did not mention the treasure.

Sébastien crouched down beside her as the two crewmen took the man and held him securely. Sébastien's dark eyes stared into hers as if he were trying to warn her of something and then the sun was blotted from her view as he dropped his head to hers and claimed her lips.

Despite her fear and her shaking body, an exquisite sweetness rushed through Madeleine's veins. Never had she felt the power that coursed through her as Sébastien's warm lips clung to hers. Instinctively her mouth opened, and she laced her arms around his neck as his tongue slowly explored her mouth. Not knowing what to do, she let her body guide her and relaxed against him. His arms went around her waist and he held her close; her legs were still trembling too much for her to stand. If she were to be honest and if she could think sensibly, the weakness in her limbs was more from the feel of Sébastien's mouth on hers than the fast diminishing fear of the man who had accosted her. Sébastien stood and pulled her up with him, his mouth not leaving hers.

Rational thought came back quickly as Madeleine opened her eyes. The man was still standing beside them and his hands were now tied behind his back. A malevolent gaze held hers and she pulled away from Sébastien.

The man knew about the necklace. He had overheard her talking to Jake. Ice replaced the warmth running through her veins as the possibility of losing everything she held dear filled her thoughts.

Chapter Thirteen

"Take him away." Sébastien held Madeleine against him as he instructed the sailors to deal with the crewman. He spoke to Jake who was now sitting up and looking around dazedly. "Are you hurt, lad?"

The African had been examining Jake's eyes and turned to face him. "He is all right. He hit his head on the keg when he was thrown across the deck. That is what caught my attention." His deep voice held authority and he held Sébastien's gaze. "He has a slight concussion and a small cut above his eye. I will see to him if that is all right with you…Captain?"

Sébastien nodded and the man helped Jake to his feet. Slowly Sébastien became aware that he was still holding Madeleine tightly to him and he eased up slightly. Her scream had awoken him, and he had run straight for the deck, not knowing what he would find. He cursed himself for allowing the crewman, Dirk, to stay aboard. From the moment the rigging had been fouled, he had had a bad feeling about the man, and he should have put him off at Barataria Bay, but the need for as many hands as he could muster had swayed his decision. He had made a wrong choice and it could have resulted in Madeleine's death.

Now he looked down at Madeleine. Her face was white, but her lips were red. Good Christ, he had an insane urge to lean down and kiss her again. His intent had been to merely stake his claim on her in front of the crew who were watching, but the simple kiss had shaken him to the core. He could still taste the sweetness of her warm lips as they had opened beneath his and welcomed him. Her soft breasts had pushed against his bare chest and the blood had rushed to his groin unbidden. Sébastien fought back a groan; he could not allow that to happen again on this voyage. There was too much at stake and he had her innocence to consider.

"I'll take you down to my cabin? Can you walk unaided?" She was trembling, and her skin was cold beneath his fingers.

Madeleine's eyes were wide, but she stepped away from his hold and nodded. "As long as I know that…that man…is confined, and will stay away from me, I shall be all right."

"You have my word. Come." He held his hand out to her and she looked at him, before curling her soft fingers in his. Sébastien tried to ignore the satisfied warmth that shot though him as she looked up at him with trust in her green eyes.

Now he had to keep her safe to keep that trust. Not only ensuring her physical safety on this mission which was fraught with danger, but safe also from the rampant desire that coursed through him every time he looked at her. Once he had Madeleine safely in his cabin, he would stay well away from her. And not only to keep her trust. He could not afford to be distracted in the days ahead or there would be more danger for all aboard this vessel.

***

Sébastien opened the door to his cabin and stood back to allow Madeleine to enter. She had waited quietly beside him while he had instructed the African man to put Jake in the small cabin adjacent to this one and watch him while he slept. His hand still held hers tightly, and his voice was kind and full of concern. Madeleine watched as the tall, dark man carried Jake into the small cabin and placed him on the bunk. His educated voice had surprised her, and she sensed that he knew what he was doing as he examined Jake's head wound. In the quick glance she had of the cabin, it showed an austere space with none of the ornate furnishings that were in the captain's cabin.

Her thoughts whirled, and she put her fingers to her brow. It was becoming more difficult for her to reconcile this kind and concerned Sébastien with the pirate captain who had pulled the assailant from her. His expression and stance had been full of barely restrained violence.

But no matter what she thought he was, she could trust him and she was safe from harm while she was on his vessel. The kiss they had just shared had firmed her certainty. It had been shared. She may be an innocent virgin, but her feminine instinct told her that he had been affected by their kiss as much as she had. Madeleine let out a small sigh of relief as Sébastien finally let go of her hand and closed the door behind them. His cabin had become a safe haven for her and at the moment she would have happily stayed below deck until the vessel berthed back at the quay in New Orleans.

He leaned back on the door and observed her without speaking as Madeleine ran a shaking hand through her hair. She needed some time to herself and she kept her voice controlled as she lifted her gaze to meet his.

"I…I'm going to have a wash." Without waiting for him to answer, she crossed to the privy and lifted the curtain to the small, private space. After it dropped behind her, she stood for a moment with her hands clenched in front of her until she heard Sébastien moving about the cabin. A clink of glass and the sound of liquid being poured preceded the scraping of a chair leg on the wooden floor and then all was quiet.

Slowly Madeleine peeled off her clothing, piece by piece until she stood naked behind the curtain. Her hands shook as she poured water from the pitcher into the bowl and soaked a wash cloth before scrubbing herself until the skin of her chest was red. She pressed the damp cloth against her face trying to let go of the fear that had filled her when the rogue crew man had grabbed her. She dipped the wash cloth in the cold water and scrubbed at her breast again to wash away the feeling of his hand against her skin.

Her thoughts were whirling—full of fear that her conversation with Jake had been overheard— but she was still confused by the reaction of her body and her traitorous emotions. Her reaction to Sébastien's kiss claiming her as his woman had set tumultuous feelings surging through her veins, even while feeling the taint of the crewman's touch.

"Madeleine, are you all right?" His voice was soft, but she knew he was close, a whisper away, just on the other side of the flimsy curtain. She grabbed for her clothes and held them against her bare breasts as Sébastien's voice came through the thin curtain.

"Are you almost done?"

"Yes, just give me a moment…please." She pressed the damp cloth against her burning cheeks and neck, and then let the cool air dry her skin for a moment before pulling her chemise back on.

After she had dressed, she quickly braided her hair and coiled it at the back of her head. She paused and swallowed before taking a deep breath and lifting the curtain.

Madeleine held her chin high and let determination flood her as she stepped out into the cabin. She had gotten herself into this situation and she would deal with it. No one else was to blame. No one else could help her.

She would ignore these strange feelings when she was in Sébastien's presence.

He stood by the table and he had put his shirt on. Madeleine hitched a thankful breath. If she'd had to look at his magnificent chest again, she did not know what she would have done.

"Come and sit with me." His expression was friendly, and his voice was calm, and a measure of confidence came back to her. Sébastien gestured to the table and she crossed the room.

"We must talk." His deep voice sent a shiver running down her back, but she nodded silently as she sat at the table. She folded her hands in her lap and she dropped her eyes, not yet ready to meet his.

"Madeleine, look at me. Don't be frightened." Sébastien's voice was kind, and she lifted her head slowly. His expression was full of concern as well as something else that she couldn't understand. No man had ever looked at her like that before, with the same hunger that was in Sébastien's eyes. She recognised it because the same need, unfamiliar yet exquisite, was still coursing through her body, overlaying her worry about the necklace and the fact that the scurrilous crewman had overhead her conversation with Jake about the diary. No matter what else was in her thoughts, Sebastian's mere presence sent the blood coursing through her veins, warming her and taking over her thoughts.

He spoke slowly, and his voice was calm as his gaze locked on hers. "I am going to speak the truth to you because I do not want you to be scared of the unknown. I deeply regret that you had to experience the attentions of that scoundrel, Dirk. I will not add to your fear by having you wonder what is going to happen in the next few days on this voyage."

Madeleine watched, fascinated as he reached his hand out across the table.

"Give me your hand."

Slowly she unclenched her fingers and slid her hand across to join with his. His thumb caressed the back of her hand as he held her gaze.

"Can I trust you, Madeleine?" His dark eyes bored into hers and she nodded. "Over the next few days I will do my utmost to ensure that there is no bloodshed on this vessel. I have a task to complete and I will be honest with you. Having you on board has made my task much more difficult."

Tears pricked at her eyes as uncertainty spiralled through her.

"But I will keep you safe." His voice lowered and was full of kindness. "Many years ago, when I was a young man I made a rash decision and a young woman lost her life. It has taken me many years to forgive myself."

"Did you love her?" Madeleine kept her voice soft, too. This was a very different man to the swaggering pirate who had teased her, frightened her, and plundered her mouth. He was trusting her with his story and a fragile connection held them together in this cabin.

Sébastien didn't answer for a few moments and her heart picked up a beat as his eyes locked with hers. Finally, he ran his hand though his hair and sighed. "I thought I did, but I believe I was too young to truly understand what I was feeling."

His voice hardened, and his dark eyes glittered. "But I will tell you now when I saw that cur with his hands on you and the knife in his hand, I thought it was going to happen all over again and I will not be placed in that position again."

Madeleine opened her eyes wide. "What? What position?"

"I was afraid he would kill you." As she looked into those dark eyes, it was the pirate who stared back at her. The man of the soft voice had disappeared, but his words belied his expression. "If he had hurt you…or Jake… I would have thrown him overboard myself."

Madeleine hitched a breath as she stared back at him. She had no doubt that this man was capable of doing just that and a shiver ran down her back. This world at sea was far removed from her quiet life in a country manor house with people at her beck and call. It was the first time in her life she had had to fight for what she wanted and her knowledge of the world, and human nature was growing. Her goal of returning to that life had been overshadowed by the fight to merely stay alive. Her fear and uncertainty must have been clear to see on her face because Sebastian pushed one of the glasses which sat in the middle of the table across to her.

"Drink of that. It will settle your nerves."

Madeleine lifted her chin higher. "I am not afraid."

"I am pleased to hear that. Courage is an admirable trait, but it would be advisable if you were a little fearful." He held her eye but while his face was expressionless, she sensed a smile was tugging at his lips. "Now drink. It will settle your nerves."

She would not allow him to see the fear deep inside her. The fear that the sailor knew her secret was overshadowed by her fear of the feelings she held for this pirate. When she was in his presence all thoughts of home and what she wanted to achieve fled from her mind. Reaching for the glass, she lifted it and watched as the golden liquid caught the light. The cut glass was heavy in her hand as she lifted it to her lips, wrinkling her nose as the sharp smell of brandy wafted across. Tipping the glass, she opened her mouth and drank the contents in one gulp. Fire burned down her throat and to her belly and she took a deep breath.

For an instant, she thought she'd surprised him as Sebastian frowned and leaned forward. She would show him she was strong and not afraid.

"May I have another?"

This time his lips did tilt in a smile as he lifted the bottle and half-filled her glass. "I suggest you sip it this time, Madeleine, as I would imagine you don't want to pass out and have me put you to bed?"

Madeleine hesitated as she lifted the glass and sensibility won out over trying to impress him with her nonchalance. She sipped and allowed the brandy to warm her before asking the question that was plaguing her thoughts.

"You assure me that man is locked away securely, and you tell me I do not have to be afraid of you, so my only concern is that I get back to New Orleans. Can you promise me that you will take me back after your…task…is done?"

"I will tell you again so that you understand me. You have no need to fear me. I will not lay a hand on you."

Madeleine bit down the angry retort that

rose to her lips. Provoking him would not get her anywhere. She would use her feminine wiles to ensure she got her own way. She knew he was far from immune to her. It may be difficult, she admitted to herself as she had no idea what they were or how to use them. She had little experience with the opposite sex; some harmless flirting with the local village boys had not prepared her for dallying with a man of his experience. Dropping her gaze, she put her hand to her forehead and let out a small troubled sigh as she relied on her instincts.

"I know that, Sébastien. You are a man I know I can trust." She let a little waver creep into her voice. "I am afraid of my fate. What will become of me after this voyage?"

"What will become of you?" An undercurrent of cynicism laced his voice. "Perhaps it is too late to think of that now. Perhaps you should have thought of that before you left the protection of your uncle's care."

It was obviously not working; she would have to try harder. Madeleine fought to keep her temper and sipped at her brandy, but it went down the wrong way and she grabbed her hand to her throat as it burned, and she coughed.

When she finally wiped the tears from her eyes, a dark gaze assessed her, and she spoke crossly, unable to hold her anger, forgetting all about feminine wiles.

"What? Why are you looking at me like that?"

"Coquetry does not become you, my dear." She glared at Sébastien as he yawned and then rose in one fluid motion. For such a large man, he was as graceful as a cat. Long limbs, sinuous movements and a currently disinterested demeanour added to his mystery. His dark eyes held hers, his long dark lashes covering his expression. His lips were full and sensuous, and she tried to forget the feel of them on hers. His face was strong, and she sensed that he may be even more determined than she when he had a goal in sight. His dark as midnight hair was pulled back from his tanned face; he truly looked like the pirate he claimed not to be.

A yawn escaped her as she watched him and weariness with her situation—or the brandy—began to cloud her mind.

Sébastien pointed to the bed. "You have had an eventful morning; I suggest you take a nap. I will get the cook to bring you something to eat." He turned to leave and Madeleine fought the disappointment that settled in her belly.

"Surely you are tired, too? I do not mind if you wish to rest?" She tried to keep her tone even.

Sébastien reached over and trailed a finger down the side of her cheek and she fought to stop her face from turning into his hand. "Being down here with you in my bed would not be a wise move, my dear."

As he walked to the door, Madeleine strained to hear the words he spoke quietly.

"I promised to keep you safe and that would certainly lead to me breaking my word."

Perhaps she had misheard. What could he mean? The door closed behind him with a soft click and Madeleine rose and crossed to the bed, confused by the feelings warring in her mind and consuming her body.

She would rest as he had suggested, and everything would seem better when she woke up.

It would.

Chapter Fourteen

Seven days passed, and Madeleine sat above deck with Jake during the day. Sébastien had not spoken to her in that time, apart from a brief acknowledgement when she came up each morning. They had fallen into a routine. She slept in the captain's cabin at night, and when she came up on deck, he disappeared for a few hours and she assumed he was sleeping in the bed she had vacated. She was anxious to return to shore; with so much time on her hands her thoughts were filled with the necklace and how she would find it and return triumphant to Bellerose.

"It appears as if we are about to see some action." Jake interrupted her daydream. "The captain and Mr. Abraham have been in conference all afternoon. The crew has guessed they are plotting co-ordinates for the intercept."

Madeleine looked around the upper and lower decks at the activity around the guns and in the rigging. Something was definitely afoot and a glimmer of anticipation ran through her. "Do you think we will be allowed to stay above deck when the...what did you call it...happens?"

"The intercept." Jake looked at her scornfully. "I will, but you will surely have to stay below deck. It may be a pirate vessel or a slave trader. There may be bloodshed." He dropped his eyes. "And beggin' your pardon. Miss Madeleine, but one look at you and they would seize you without hesitation." Jake's face was scarlet.

"Yes, Madeleine." Sébastien's deep voice came from behind her and she jumped as his voice set her nerve endings firing all over her body. She had not heard him approach. She would have to take care with what she said in future when she believed she and Jake were alone. Sébastien walked as silently as a ghost.

"The lad speaks the truth. It is time for you to go below deck." Sébastien waited for her to move.

Madeleine stood and pulled the top of her chemise up as she rose. This tight fitting attire was unfamiliar. It seemed to have a mind of its own and she constantly had to remember to check she was not indecently displaying too much bare flesh. She looked across at Jake.

"Whatever is about to happen, you keep

yourself safe." She reached across and brushed a quick kiss across his cheek and Jake's face coloured even more. "You are the only friend I have."

Sébastien's eyes were on her and his mouth was set in a straight line.

"Why are you looking at me like that?" Madeleine put her hands on her hips and looked up at him. His white shirt was loose and billowing in the stiff breeze and his hair had come loose from the leather at the back of his neck. Despite that, Sébastien's expression was stern and she ignored the little frisson of fear that snaked down her spine.

"I am merely waiting for you to follow me. I am not aware of any 'look' on my face that is different to usual." He spoke formally and gestured for her to step ahead of him. She shot a final smile to Jake and mouthed a farewell to him before she turned to the hatch.

Sébastien followed her down the ladder and ushered her into the cabin as she fought the panic rising in her chest. She sensed impatience in him, a suppressed excitement, as he stood at the open door and regarded her solemnly. His brow was furrowed, and his usually arched eyebrows were set in a straight line. She stared back at him as his dark eyes held hers and the panic dissipated as the usual warm heat rushed to her belly.

When he spoke, the deep timbre of his voice set the pulse pounding in her throat. She had missed the parry and thrust of their conversations since he had been avoiding her for the past week.

"I would remind you of my request. You must stay below deck." His gaze bored into hers and Madeleine parted her lips as she took in a deep breath. His eyes followed the movement and a small measure of satisfaction filled her. He was not immune to her.

"Jake is right. We are now to the part of our voyage which is fraught with danger." He reached out and where his hand settled on her bare shoulder, Madeleine's skin burned.

"I have no doubt all will be well, but it is imperative you stay below deck. Can I trust you to do as I ask?"

"I will." She nodded. "I promise you."

"I will not lock you in. In case there is a fire—but rest assured—there is little chance of that."

Madeleine held his gaze as she nodded. A curse left Sébastien's lips.

"For luck." He reached out and pulled her close. His lips descended on hers in a hard, swift kiss before he pulled back and looked at her.

Madeleine lifted her fingers to her lips and whispered. "Stay safe, Sébastien."

He turned on his heel and walked to the door and Madeleine thought he was going to leave without a backward glance at her. As she held her fingers to her lips trying to keep the warmth from his lips, he turned slowly, and his gaze lingered on her face. Madeleine yearned for him to stay with her. She lowered her hand from her mouth and held it out to him, but he turned and stepped through the door before closing it quietly behind him.

"Please God, keep them both safe." Madeleine muttered the words and her voice broke. For the first time since her family's untimely deaths, she worried about the safety of another.

Jake, her young friend. And Sébastien, a pirate captain, whom she trusted with her life, if not her heart.

***

Her simple but heartfelt words filled his mind as Sébastien stood on the upper deck with Mr. Abrahams and looked to the south.

Stay safe. He had no fear for his physical safety but was fighting the feelings that filled him when he was in Madeleine's presence and when he thought of her well-being. As long as he could keep her safe and return her safely to…

To who? That was a problem to be dealt with when the goals of this mission had been achieved. It would be necessary to find out more about her personal circumstances. He shook his head and lifted his hands to the back of his neck, quickly securing the loose hair into a short braid before winding the leather tie around the end.

A boiling mass of clouds was just visible above the horizon as the dark of night began to descend suddenly as it did out near the islands which he knew were close by.

"There will be no moon before we reach the Ann Marie." Mr. Abraham's voice was low.

"Yes, and with any luck the storm will be upon us just as we reach her."

"Captain!' The shrill cry came down from above and they both looked up. The sailor manning the platform was pointing to the east. "There she is."

A flurry of activity followed as the crew took on their respective roles. The master gunner gathered his four crewmen together ready to load, aim, fire, and reset the guns as needed. Sailors climbed the rigging, ready to drop the extra sails to pick up speed as soon as it was pitch dark.

Sébastien smiled as he beckoned Jake over

to him. It was fortuitous that they had come across the Ann Marie in the dark of night. It would make for a greater surprise, and the boarding and the transfer would be so much easier. So close to their final destination, the captain of the slave trader would be complacent as he approached San Domingo. Sébastien knew these waters like the back of his hand. He had learned how to sail in the Caribbean Sea.

"Jake. I have a task for you."

"Yes, Captain?" The young lad looked up at him earnestly.

"I want you to go down to Miss Madeleine and ensure that she is informed that the ship is to be in total darkness. She must not have her lantern alight."

"Yes, Captain."

Before the cabin boy could scurry away to the ladder, Sébastien stayed him with a hand to his shoulder. "After that, I want you to send up the crewman who is guarding the door of the brig and I want you to take over guard duty below deck" He knew the lad would be safer down there than up on deck if anything went awry and there was little fear of the prisoner escaping. Sébastien had himself checked his bindings on his way up to the deck.

"Yes, Captain."

Sébastien's muscles tensed as the boy

disappeared and the ship was shrouded in silent darkness. The next hour was crucial and the success of the mission hinged on the element of surprise. Their sails had been furled as the time for the intercept had come closer and he was sure that the other vessel would not have seen them against the glare of the setting sun. Anticipation filled him. It was almost time. He grinned as he caught himself making the sign of the cross on his chest. Sébastien was not a religious man but his entire future depended on the success of this mission. The *Maiden* sliced silently through the small swells of the waves as the storm clouds boiled ahead of them.

Chapter Fifteen

Madeleine hoped when the events of the night were over, and all went to Sébastien's plan, they would be returning to New Orleans. She would have to find some new clothing before she could step off the *Maiden* and finish her quest. For some reason, the urgency of the need for her to complete her quest and return home had dimmed. She pushed that thought away, not wanting to dwell on what had diminished her determination.

As she lay there, the gentle rocking of the boat soothed her and she let her mind wander to Great Aunt Josephine's diary. A small shiver ran down her spine as she thought of the crewman, Dirk, who knew of the existence of the necklace. Perhaps she would have to tell Sébastien a little about her quest to ensure that the man did not follow her when she finally got back to New Orleans. She knew Sébastien was a good man and she could trust him.

Perhaps he would even help me? I could pay him and then he could assist me to find a passage home. The thought of saying goodbye to him left a strange feeling in her chest and she swallowed it down.

I catch my breath and throb with need as I wait for his skilful touch. Aunt Josephine's words held new meaning for her now and Madeleine had a deeper understanding of what Josephine had been feeling when she had penned them. With a simple kiss or two, Sébastien had touched her in places she had never felt before and her mind wandered over the pleasures that Aunt Josephine had described. Her skin tingled as she imagined Sébastien's fingers stroking her as she had read about in the diary.

What pleasures unheard of, undreamed of? She closed her eyes and hitched a breath; she could almost feel his fingers on her skin.

Boom! The sound reverberated around the cabin and Madeleine sat upright, her hands over her ears. The boat rocked from side to side and gathered speed as Mr. Abrahams' shouted command to drop the sails reached her through the timber deck. Loud voices and the sound of running feet were followed by another loud boom.

"Oh, God, please keep Sébastien safe."

Madeleine jumped from the bed and pulled her skirt on over her chemise. She stepped to the narrow window at the end of the cabin and hesitantly pressed her face to the opening. It was too dark to see anything apart from some lights ahead of them to the port side of the boat. The lights were getting closer.

A bloodcurdling scream was followed by a loud grating noise and the vessel shuddered and came to a stop. The metallic clanking of what she assumed were cutlasses reached her, soon followed by another loud explosion. The unlit lamp next to the bed fell to the floor and shattered with a loud smash, and then all was quiet.

Be safe, Sébastien. She knew Jake was below deck so she had no need to worry about his safety.

"Reset, reset, reset," someone yelled and the urgency in their voice made her catch her breath.

A second and louder boom shook the *Maiden* and the acrid smell of gunpowder filled the cabin. The timber of the hull creaked and groaned as the boat came up hard against another vessel. Madeleine lost her balance and fell to the floor, grazing her knee. Then all was still, and the sounds faded away to silence again as the boat rocked gently from side to side.

She felt her way back through the cabin in the pitch darkness, her chest heavy with worry as she wondered what was happening on the deck. She was concerned about the blood curdling scream she had heard. Reaching the privy, she held the curtain up and stepped inside, wishing it was not so dark. She felt around for the bowl of water to bathe her knee where the wooden floor had pierced her skin. Her right knee was stinging and she could feel the blood running down her leg.

Madeleine took a step forward and cried out as a rough shard of porcelain pierced the skin beneath her foot. The wash bowl must have fallen and smashed into pieces on the floor. Afraid to move another step on her bare feet for fear of stepping on more broken china, she stood with her hand over her mouth debating whether to pick the pieces up by feel, and risk cutting her hands, or to try and step out into the cabin without cutting her feet again.

As Madeleine stood there in the dark deciding which course of action to take, the cabin door unlatched, and she let out a sigh of relief. It had to be either Jake or Sébastien and they could pass her shoes to her if they were able to find them in the dark.

Please let it be Sébastien. She wanted to

ensure he was all right after the ruckus on the deck. Madeleine's heart began to pound in slow heavy beats as an unfamiliar voice reached her.

Two voices, as the first one was immediately answered by a second deeper voice.

"She must be asleep in the bed." The harsh whisper turned her blood to ice. She didn't recognise the heavily accented voice, but knew it had to be one of the crew. If it was someone from the other boat, they wouldn't know she was down here in the captain's cabin. She stifled a gasp; perhaps they knew that Sébastien was hurt—or worse—and would not be coming down here.

"Don't kill her just yet. We have to find that diary." The harsh whisper reached her and she froze, afraid to make a sound or a movement.

"If it is not easily found, we shall have to threaten her, so she tells us where it is."

"There are not many hiding places down here." The accented voice was terse. "Damn it all, I wish I could find the lantern."

Please, God. If they were unfamiliar with the cabin, they would not know there was a curtained alcove on the other side of the entry door. The footsteps moved away from her in the dark

"It's too dark. I can't see a blasted thing." The frustration was evident in his voice. "Where is the bed?"

"Ssh." The other man hissed. "Don't wake her up. The last thing we need is the captain down here. She has him bewitched."

Thank God. Sébastien must be all right, just occupied by the melee above.

The sound of a body landing on the bed was followed by a grunt of frustration. "She's not there."

"Then where in God's name would she be?"

"I don't know." The heavily accented voice got louder, and Madeleine breathed a sigh of relief. Perhaps they would assume she was no longer in the cabin.

"There is no way he would have allowed her above deck," the first man said.

"Do you have your flint? Shed some light here and we will see if there is a lantern by the bed."

Madeleine bit her lip and tried to recall the layout of the small space she was in. There was a small space behind the stand that held the pitcher and wash bowl. The problem was, if she tried to get to it and stood on some broken shards of the bowl, it would crunch beneath her feet and the intruders would hear her and discover her hiding place. Her heart beat accelerated and her mouth dried.

"You search here, and I'll look in the other cabins. The captain would not have put her in the other end with Dirk. She has to be in here or in the next cabin. She may have been afeared by the action up above and is hiding." There was an evil laugh and her blood iced in her veins as the man spoke. "If you are hiding, my sweet, you should be afeared, as you know what pirates do to buxom wenches."

The door opened and closed, and the next minute there was a flash of light as the remaining man struck his flint and the sweet smell of burning camphene reached her as the wick fizzed into life. He had found the lamp on the table.

Madeleine knew she had to move and hide now, or it would be too late. He would reach this end of the cabin quickly. She prayed that the space was large enough for her to be shielded from his view. Silently she slid one foot backward, waiting for the tell-tale noise as her foot hit a piece of the bowl. But there was nothing. Slowly, she slid her other foot back to join it. Still nothing; she had managed to avoid the broken shards. The light was getting closer and she heard a triumphant cry as the intruder found the alcove she had hidden in on her first night on the *Maiden*.

"Damnation, where are you girl? I will find you. There is no fear of that."

From somewhere deep within, Madeleine found the courage to swing around behind the stand and drop to a crouch. She tucked her arms and legs up tightly against her body and watched as the shadow from the lantern danced on the wall above her head. She closed her eyes and waited to be found, but before he reached the end of the room the door opened and there was an indignant cry.

"What are you doing in Miss Madeleine's cabin?" Jake shouted. "What have you done with her, you scurrilous dog?"

Madeleine stayed silent and did not move as she heard Jake run up the corridor to the ladder. He'd obviously left the door open and the second man returned almost immediately.

"Quickly. Get out of here before the captain comes down. We will have to find it on the way back to port."

There was a scurry of hurried footsteps as they departed and then all was quiet. Madeleine finally gave in to her fear and let the tears roll down her cheeks as she stayed hidden in the small aperture.

***

Sébastien lifted his hand in farewell as the

French trader sailed away from his vessel, although he doubted whether his new African friend could see him in the dark. The transition of the fifteen slaves on the *Maiden* to the Ann Marie had been flawless, once the French captain had realised he was outnumbered. Dawn was an hour away and the foray in the dead of the night had been most successful. There had been little bloodshed and no fatalities, although he grimaced as he raised his other hand to his shoulder to staunch the slowly seeping blood where a cutlass had nicked him. Sébastien took a deep breath of the fresh, sweet air as his crew prepared to turn the vessel around and set sail for home. They had taken no booty as the slave trader had not carried any. The Ann Marie had had a full cargo of slaves who were now en route back to their homeland across the Atlantic Ocean. The French captain was safely below decks of the *Maiden* and would be treated well until he was released into the care of Governor Carondelet. It was Sebastien's small contribution toward the ending of the huge slave trade to San Domingo where he had been born. For a time, he had considered going back home to the island of his birth to start his own plantation but since the French had taken control last year, he would not return. The island had been in anarchy since the second Treaty of Basel when the Spanish had relinquished the last of the island to the French.

There were also too many sad memories there. Sébastien preferred to leave those behind.

The Hawaiian Islands beckoned and now that this mission was over, and successful, it would be a reality for him. The only thing remaining was to safely deposit Madeleine back to her uncle—Sébastien frowned as he wondered if that was the right thing to do—and collect his payment from the governor. He looked over to the horizon where the first pink tinge stained the sky and hinted at the dawn of a new day. On the morrow, he would ensure Madeleine was up on the deck with him to witness the sunrise.

Chapter Sixteen

"Captain, Captain!" Jake's shrill cry reached Sébastien as he dipped a cloth into the barrel of fresh water on the lower deck to dab his shoulder. His wound was not serious but needed cleansing before he put his shirt on and went below deck to check on Madeleine. He turned quickly at the distress in the lad's voice as he jumped from the top of the ladder at the hatch. As Jake ran down to Sébastien, two figures emerged from the hatch and slipped into the shadows behind the wheelhouse. Sébastien frowned and dropped the cloth, grabbing the boy by his shoulders.

"What is it?"

"Captain, you must come quickly. Miss Madeleine is missing and there is an intruder in your cabin." Jake's eyes were wide, and his voice shook. He bent double taking deep breaths.

All of Sébastien's worst nightmares came to the forefront of his thoughts as he threw the cloth to the deck and ran for the ladder. He paused and put his hand to his eyes before he stepped through the hatch; he could just make out the billowing sails of the Ann Marie on the horizon. If they had to give chase, he took note of the direction but for the life of him he could not imagine how they could have gotten Madeleine onto the trader without him noticing.

Hurrying down the ladder, he paused at the bottom and put his fingers up to his lips, indicating for Jake to be silent. Slowly and quietly, he made his way to the cabin and stepped thought the open door. He looked around; the lamp from the table beside the bed was in pieces on the floor, yet the lamp on the table was burning brightly. All was quiet; the room was empty and apart from the broken lamp all looked as it should. There was no sign of anyone in the cabin. He circled around and checked the alcove in the hull, praying that Madeleine was in there, but when he lifted the curtain, the small space was empty and the blanket was folded neatly.

Guilt swamped through him. It had happened again; he had lost a woman. An innocent young woman who had asked for nothing more than to be free of her tyrannical uncle. In that instant, Sébastien realised that if he found Madeleine, he would not be turning her over to that devil dodger.

Please God, if he found her safely, he would find a safe place for her in New Orleans. Surely the governor's wife would know of a family she could board with until he sorted out her future. Putting his fingers to his lips once more, he indicated to Jake to remain quiet as Sébastien approached the curtained privy at the other end of the large cabin. He stepped back and slowly opened the curtain, half-expecting the intruder to be hiding in there.

But it was empty like the rest of the cabin.

His shoulders slumped, and he beckoned Jake into the room. "Tell me exactly what happened, Jake. What did you see? Did you see them take Miss Madeleine?" Even as Sébastien spoke he realised that they would not have had time to get her from below by the time Jake had summoned him on the upper deck.

"There was only one man and he—"

"I'm in here." A small voice interrupted Jake's explanation and Sébastien whirled around.

"Madeleine?"

"Yes." The reply came from low in the cabin.

"Where are you?"

"I'm in the privy and it is most unpleasant." Her voice was more confident now. "Can you get my slippers please?"

"Your slippers?"

"Yes, your ship steering skills leave a lot to be desired. The floor is littered with broken china. I need my slippers please."

Sébastien opened the curtain once more and the light from the lamp reflected on the broken blue and white shards of the pitcher and bowl that had once graced the cupboard in the privy. She was not in there.

"Where the deuce are you?" The top of Jake's head brushed his elbow as he peered around Sébastien into the seemingly empty space.

"I'm behind the privy and it's not very pleasant."

Utter relief coursed through Sébastien and he burst out laughing.

"It's not funny. I think I'm stuck."

"Jake, pass me the lamp, please and see if you can find Miss Madeleine's slippers." Sébastien fought back the laughter that threatened to break out once more. He knew it was more from relief that she was alive and safe rather than her current predicament.

"Here you are, Captain." Jake held the lamp high and passed him a pair of wooden-soled silk slippers laced up with colourful ribbons on each side.

"Would you like me to unlace your shoes before I pass them in?"

"Yes, please." For the first time, Madeleine's voice was meek.

It only took Sébastien a few minutes to unlace the slippers and pass them in, and then for Madeleine to emerge bottom-first from the narrow space. He placed his hands firmly on either side of her skirts and guided her out, trying to ignore the pleasure of holding her.

She straightened and nodded with an almost regal incline of her head. "Thank you."

"What's wrong with your foot?" Sébastien watched as Madeleine reached down and slipped off one of her shoes before she hobbled over to the bed.

"I stood on a broken shard when I was hiding."

She looked back at him and her eyes narrowed. "What's wrong with your shoulder? You're bleeding, too."

Sébastien put his hand over the small wound on his shoulder. "Just a small flesh wound. Nothing to worry about."

Jake hovered by the door and Sébastien smiled at him. "Lad, would you please go above deck and bring down a pitcher of fresh water. Mr. Abrahams will show you where it is."

Jake hurried off, looking pleased to be trusted with a task for the captain. Sébastien crossed to the chest at the end of the bed and opened the lid to survey the contents. He reached in and lifted a handful of fabric as he searched for a suitable cloth to use to wash Madeleine's foot when Jake returned.

"So tell me—" he kept his voice light "—do you know why the scoundrel was in my cabin and what he was looking for?"

Madeleine raised her head and met his gaze squarely. Her eyes locked with his and a strange feeling shot through Sébastien. It was more than relief that she was unharmed; it was more of a deep connection that linked them together. A shared concern for the other's safety and a quiet satisfaction in each other's presence filled the silence, something that he had never experienced before. He dropped the lid of the chest and crossed to the bed where Madeleine was sitting, her eyes still on him. Carefully placing the cloths on the bed, he sat beside her and looked down at her hands, held still in her lap. He let his gaze travel up her arms, her bare skin glowing softly in the lamp light.

"I would never have forgiven myself if anything had happened to you. I should have left someone down here with you to ensure your safety."

Her chin lifted a little. "I was able to look after myself, Captain. I told you I was capable of that."

Sébastien reached down and picked up one of her hands and held it between his. "Yes, you did. You are a very brave and determined young woman."

As he spoke, he realised that Madeleine was very different to Lisette. As well as being willing to look after herself, her concern for others was clear to see. Even as the thought crossed his mind, she lifted her free hand and touched his shoulder.

"You have more than a small wound. It needs attention. Will you let me take care of it for you?"

Her voice was soft, and he raised his head and chanced a look at her face. Her eyes held his as her soft fingers stayed on his shoulder.

"We are a fine pair, Sébastien."

"That we are, Madeleine." The temptation of her expression defeated his good intentions. He lowered his head and claimed her mouth before she had even closed her lips. It was impossible not to. Her lips clung to his and a small moan escaped her. Sébastien held her hand against his chest, certain she could feel his heart racing. She pulled her hand from his and splayed her fingers against his chest. A shiver of excitement rippled through Sébastien as her tongue tentatively sought his. He increased the pressure of his lips as her soft mouth welcomed him, and slowly and gently he pushed her back onto the bed. Reaching down, he gently slid his hand along her thigh and the fabric of his breeches strained against his erection as she lifted herself to push herself against his hand.

Dropping his hand lower, he encountered bare skin and ran his fingers along her knee and slowly up her silky thigh.

Another moan escaped her lips and as she pulled her mouth from his, a measure of sanity returned to him.

"I'm sorry. I did not mean to frighten you." He sat up and dropped his head into his hands.

"Don't be sorry. There is no need."

He risked a glance at Madeleine and then immediately wished he hadn't. Her lips were full and red, and her cheeks were rosy, but it was the slumberous desire in her eyes that echoed in her words.

"I was simply afraid that Jake would come back…and I would have been embarrassed for him to see me like that." She pulled her skirt down where it had slid up her thigh and Sébastien clenched his fingers, so he did not touch her again.

"And Sébastien?" He raised his eyes to hers. "I was not afraid. Perhaps we can explore—"

She stopped speaking as the sound of Jake's feet hitting the floor at the bottom of the ladder reached them only seconds before he pushed the door open.

Good Christ. If she hadn't pulled back, he would have been on top of her by now, exploring the satiny skin beneath his fingers, ravishing her.

An innocent...and a virgin. He was sure of that.

What had she been going to say? Perhaps we can explore what? Maybe she was not as innocent as he thought? All he knew was that whenever he was near her, he could not think with a clear head.

"Captain." Jake opened the door and carefully held out a pitcher of water and then awaited instructions from the captain.

"I am sure Mr. Abrahams is in need of help now that we have lost some of our crew." He walked to the door to Jake and lowered his voice. "Please tell Mr. Abrahams that I will be resting. . .and Jake?"

"Yes, Captain?

"Please ask him to keep a close eye on the new crew members. I may be wrong, but I suspect that they may be in league with the man who attacked Miss Madeleine the other day."

"Yes, sir. Is there anything else?"

"No, Jake...I will call you if I need anything else." The lad looked up at him and then across at Madeleine who was sitting up on the bed, her foot hanging over the edge.

"Is Miss Madeleine all right?"

"Yes, lad, that she is and I thank you for your loyalty. You shall be rewarded once we get to shore."

Jake shook his head as he stepped to the door. "There is no need for reward, sir. It is a part of my duty...and a part of my friendship with Miss Madeleine.

"Then you are a true friend indeed."

Sébastien closed the door and dropped the latch before he turned slowly to face Madeleine, his gut churning with uncertainty. How could a mere slip of a girl create these feelings of confusion? Anger flared in his chest.

By God, I'm the captain of this vessel and I will begin to act like one, not like some love-struck young fool. Not again.

***

Sébastien stood by the door holding the pitcher of water that Jake had delivered, and sympathy shot through Madeleine when she saw his grim expression. As he caught her eye, he dropped his eyes, avoiding her intent examination.

Confidence and trust filled her as she watched him but he walked across to the table and put the pitcher down without looking back at her. He straightened his shoulders and looked at her, his face unsmiling.

"I will attend to your foot and then we will talk about what happened."

"When Jake interrupted?"

"No." His jaw was set and his voice terse. He shot her a glance as he dipped one of the cloths into the pitcher of water before walking over to where she sat.

He looked at the bed as though it were a snake about to strike him and Madeleine smothered a smile as a surge of feminine power filled her chest. Despite keeping his face set, he was not in control; even with her lack of experience she knew that. A pulse ticked in his cheek and her instinct told her he was as unsettled in her company as she was in his.

"We will talk about what happened before you hid in the privy."

How much can I tell him? Madeleine knew only too well what those two crewmen had been searching for, but still she was unsure of how much to tell Sébastien.

Can I trust him? Can I tell him why I need to find Aunt Josephine's house? Or is he not really who I think he is? She swallowed and decided to tell him the bare bones of her story if he asked again.

"Hold this." Sébastien held out the damp cloth to her. He crouched in front of her and gently lifted her foot, cradling it in his hand as he examined it. She turned her ankle slightly, so he could see the cut, and drew in her breath as his gentle fingers probed along the arch of her foot.

"Ow." Madeleine jerked her leg back. "That hurts."

Triumphantly, he held up a small piece of porcelain. "I believe this is the culprit." He pulled her foot to him again before holding his hand out for the cloth. His head bowed in concentration as he gently pressed the cloth against the cut on her foot.

"So, begin with what happened and tell me what you heard." Finally, he lifted his head and looked at her. Madeleine put her hand to her mouth and her mind ticked over as she observed him. Was she being naïve just because her body ran rampant every time Sébastien was close? She would swear if he kissed her again, she would probably faint with the delight of it.

God forbid, if he touched her again.

His eyes were kind as she took his measure. Usually dark and glittering, she stared into his pupils and leaned closer to Sébastien. Today his eyes were of a warm, dark brown and the flecks in his irises matched the golden skin of his bare chest. She leaned closer and the heat of him seemed to warm her even with distance between them. With a stifled groan he took her hands and held them tightly in his grip.

"Do you realise how you look at me?" His voice was husky. "It does not befit a single young woman in mourning."

Madeleine allowed a slow smile to cross her face while she held his gaze steadily. Then she dropped her eyes to her chest and gestured with a casual flick of her hand to her attire. "Does it befit a pirate's wench?"

"Enough." He dropped her hands and rose swiftly to his feet and strode across the cabin to the table. "Come away from the bed and sit with me here before you entice me to actions I will long regret. You are an innocent, Madeleine, and you do not know the power of your charm. You are playing with fire and you will get hurt." He pulled out one of the chairs and waited for her. "Are you able to walk on your injured foot?"

"Yes." Her voice was sulky as she crossed to the table. Who was he to tell her she would get hurt? He knew nothing about her and even if his assumptions about her innocence may have been correct, he did not need to know that. If he believed her to be more experienced than she was, he may trust her enough to let her go ashore alone when they berthed in New Orleans.

***

"Who was in my cabin? Tell me what was said."

The petulant set to Madeleine's lips reminded Sébastien of Lisette when she wanted her own way. It amused Sébastien but he would not give in to her. It took his attention momentarily from the pressure in his breeches. Sitting beside her on his bed had brought all manner of tempting—and inappropriate—thoughts to his mind. "Did they say what they were looking for? Or God forbid, do you believe they were looking for you?"

It seemed peculiar to him that the assailants would choose that time to go looking for a woman…and the woman who was known as the pirate's woman. They were sure to know that they would end up overboard when he discovered them with her. It made no sense.

"They were looking for something that I

do not have." Madeleine crossed her arms in front of her chest and her loose chemise dropped from one shoulder exposing her bare, white skin.

Holy Mother of Christ. Sébastien closed his eyes for a moment and took a deep breath. "So if you do not have it, how did they know what they sought?"

"The other man—the one who is locked up— heard me telling a…story…to Jake. He— that man— must have told them."

"What sort of story?" He had not known her long, but he knew her well enough to know when she was lying…or avoiding the truth. She dropped her gaze to her folded arms.

"Madeleine?"

"A story about something that I would like to have one day. Something that by rights belongs to me."

"Tell me about it."

"I can't." Her voice was firm.

"You can tell Jake about it? But not me?" A tinge of jealousy shot through Sébastien before he realised it was ridiculous to be jealous of her friendship with the young lad. "Why not me, Madeleine? You can trust me with your secret."

"Can I, Sébastien?" Her gaze was steadfast as she stared at him. "You? A pirate who is after booty and fortune?"

Unease roiled in his stomach. Was that how this beautiful young woman thought of him? For the first time in many years, it mattered to him that he was not thought to be a dishonest and self-serving man. It had suited his purposes while he earned enough to leave this all behind, but he did not want Madeleine to think poorly of him. Why that bothered him, he did not know.

He reached across the table, picked up her small white hand and entwined her fingers in his. She did not pull away and a measure of satisfaction shot through him.

God help me. Even the touch of her fingers in his sent fire racing through his veins.

"I am an honest man, Madeleine. I am not a pirate." Her wide green eyes held his and in that instant, he decided to tell her everything. "I will trust you. Because I want you to know. What I will tell you no one else knows. Only the Spanish governor."

"The governor? He approves of what you do?

Sébastien nodded slowly. "Not only does he approve, he sends me on these missions. For the past two years, I have earned enough freeing slaves from slave traders' vessels that I can now leave."

"Leave where?" Her face was alight with curiosity and he was pleased she was interested in his story.

"When we dock in New Orleans, I will leave the *Maiden* under the command of Mr. Abrahams. I will not return to the sea."

Madeleine's brow furrowed. "Haven't you always been a sea captain? What will you do?"

Sébastien turned her hand over and gently traced the lines on her palm as he reminisced. "I grew up on a beautiful island. A lush, green island where soft breezes blew, and the smell of the sea was always around. Not far from where we sail now. My grandfather owned a sugar plantation on San Domingo and I learned all there was to know about growing sugar as I worked by his side."

"So you will go back to this island you speak of?" She tipped her head to the side as she waited for his answer.

He lifted his chin and stared past her. "No, there are other islands far from here where I shall make a new beginning." The memories on San Domingo were memories he did not want to keep. His mother and Lisette were both buried in the town and the family plantation had been sold to fund Jean-Luc's gambling debts.

No, Sébastien wanted to be far from all of

that.

"The Hawaiian Islands. That is where my future lies."

Chapter Seventeen

Madeleine could see the longing on Sébastien's face as he spoke of a new beginning and a new life. For the first time since she had left home, her determination began to waver. The importance of finding the necklace and returning to England with her grand plan to restore the family estate had lessened. The ways in the New World seemed to be very different to the way of life she was well used to on the estate in Derbyshire. Sébastien spent his days freeing slaves from a life of servitude, while she was trying to find the necklace, so she could bring the people from her village back to work on the family estate. Jake's thoughts about servants the other day had made her think deeply about what she was doing, and she began to wonder whether her motives were selfish.

Perhaps it is not so different from the slavery over here in the New World? But it was all she had ever known. A small sound of distress escaped her lips as her thoughts whirled around in confusion.

"What's wrong?" Sébastien squeezed her fingers gently. "I did not mean to upset you."

Madeleine lifted her head. His expression was kind and she imagined for a brief moment that perhaps it was more than concern for her well-being that brought that softness to his face. She held his gaze and the light caught the golden flecks in his deep brown eyes.

"There were two men." Taking a deep breath, she rushed on before she changed her mind. She would trust him. "They were looking for a diary that belonged to my…family."

"A diary? Is it here in my cabin?" Sébastien frowned and looked around as though he expected to see it lying out in full view.

"No. No, it is in England. It is in the library at Bellerose Hall—my home." She shook her head and hitched a sob. "Or rather, what used to be my home."

Sébastien let go of her hand and stood, before walking around slowly to where she sat at the table. He kept his gaze on her as he crouched beside her. "I think you had better start at the beginning and tell me your whole story."

The words poured from Madeleine as she

told him of leaving her home with Uncle Titus after he had stripped it bare, of the planned marriage and how she had been determined to escape him. She fought the tears that pressed at the back of her eyes as she described her home to Sébastien and explained how her parents and brother had been killed, and how Uncle Titus had taken over her life.

Sébastien stood and took her hands, pulling her up to her feet before his arms encircled her. Madeleine sighed as he held her close and she rested her head on his shoulder. His chest vibrated against her as he spoke.

"I knew you were brave, but I did not realise how truly courageous you are."

"That's not all. Uncle Titus took me ashore and I met a man who I was supposed to marry. A man who seemed more interested in where my aunt lived, than taking a wife."

She lifted her head and raised her hand to his shoulder. His skin was wet from her tears and she trailed her fingers over his chest as he looked down at her.

"I thought if I came here and found—"

She broke off and swallowed as he waited for her to finish.

"Found what, Madeleine?"

"Found the heirloom that was in the diary, I thought I could go back to my home and everything would be the way it was. But now, I don't know if it is the right course of action." Lifting her chin, she held his gaze. "My father's aunt lived here, and she hid a necklace in her house. She wrote of it in her diary—I am the only relative left, other than Uncle Titus, that is. I spoke to Jake of the diary and the necklace and we were overheard." She felt herself tremble as fear spiked through her. "It seems that others know of the diary...or the necklace. Foolishly, I thought I would just come to New Orleans, find Aunt Josephine's house, collect it, and all would be well.

"I will deal with the men who were in my cabin when we get to New Orleans. If I lock more men up, the crew will be uneasy." His voice was soft. "But you must forget all about finding this treasure you seek. It is too dangerous for a young woman such as you to be embarking on such a quest."

"I do not agree. Why would you say that?" A weight settled on Madeleine's shoulders; yet another impediment to block her path. She folded her arms and lifted her chin.

"I will help you before I seek passage to the islands. But only to see you safely on your way to England before I depart. You must forget all about this necklace. You have my word I will help you go home."

"No." Madeleine stood on her toes and softly kissed Sébastien's cheek to soften her words. The stubble of his cheek was rough beneath her lips and his soft groan sent a pleasurable ripple through her. "I may take your offer of assistance after I succeed in finding my family's heirloom."

"You cannot follow this foolish idea of yours. Trust me when I say it is too dangerous."

"I must."

"Why must you?"

"I've already told you." Madeleine tried to keep the conviction in her voice. "I must get the necklace to help them all back home in Derbyshire."

Sébastien held her arms and shook his head. "You must forget that foolish idea. You are a most frustrating young woman. I promised to keep you safe but I think you may be more at risk of harm from me when you look at me with your emerald eyes."

She shook her head at the frown that crossed his brow, even as his touch sent thrills coursing through her blood. "You are truly a good man. I am sorry I doubted your motives." For a moment, her frustration with Sébastien for dismissing her determination to find the necklace was overshadowed by the thought of saying good bye to him at the end of the voyage. "But I cannot agree with you...about the necklace."

"Madeleine, you do not know what you do to me." Sébastien stared at her and a rush of warmth filled her belly and as it travelled lower, her legs trembled.

Even when she had thought him to be a pirate, this man had fascinated her. And now that she knew the truth of Sébastien, it would be so hard to leave him. She could not ignore the pleasurable feelings that coursed through her body when he was near her. The pleasure of simply being in his company would stay with her for a long time. She raised her hand to her lips where the taste of his skin still lingered.

"And you to me, Sébastien." The words that were in her head left her lips before she could hold them back. "I want you."

***

Sébastien's gaze trailed down past Madeleine's bare shoulders to the soft swell of her breasts. Courageous and determined, she was beautiful; the strongest woman he had ever met. There was no doubt of her fair-skinned beauty, but for Sébastien it was Madeleine's inner beauty that shone through. She knew what she wanted, and she had held onto her convictions, no matter what danger she was in. And he had tried hard to dissuade her from this foolish and dangerous quest.

I want you. Her words filled his head; but his desire overcame his attempt to rationalize the foolishness of touching her, to resist taking her innocence. Sébastien was helpless beneath the sway of her emerald gaze. She leaned her head back as his fingers lifted her heavy auburn tresses from her neck, and bared her neck to his lips. His other hand slipped through the folds of her skirt and ran slowly up the outside of her bare thigh and when she let out a soft groan Sébastien was lost.

Her skin was soft and warm, and he stayed his hand before it reached the top of her leg. He slid his lips up her graceful neck and lightly licked her skin. Her skin tasted of the sweet fragrance that came from her hair—like the roses his mother had picked from her garden when he was a child. The memory of home flitted though his mind and he pulled back.

What the hell am I doing? I should be keeping her safe. He pulled back, slowly shaking his head and pulled his hand away from her bare thigh, but Madeleine dropped her hand over his and pressed it against her leg.

"Please. It is all right. I want you to touch me." Her slumberous eyes looked up at him and Sébastien was torn. Despite her request, he could see the nervousness in her beautiful emerald eyes. Did she know that her needs were the same as his? But she was untouched and innocent, and he should not be thinking these thoughts.

"Sébastien." Her voice was low and husky. "I want you. I want you in every way a woman wants a man. I may know nothing, and you will have to guide me, but it is what I want." She turned her head and pressed her lips against his and he groaned against her mouth. "It is what I need."

Sliding her hand around to the front of his breeches, Madeleine pressed her hand against the hardness that was throbbing there, almost unbearably. He had never wanted a woman with such ferocity. Before he could move, she dropped her other hand and unlaced his breeches without taking her lips from his. Warm soft fingers encircled his bare flesh and he was lost.

He lifted her hands above her head and spoke against her lips, pushing his doubt aside. "Madeleine, I will be gentle with you, I swear."

"I know. Take me to your bed."

His fingers ran though her luxuriant auburn tresses and he was surrounded by the sweet rose smell. Sébastien deepened the pressure of his kiss and as her mouth opened beneath his, he kissed her slowly. He would not rush this, her first time. Promises of exquisite pleasure, words of reassurance interspersed his kisses and finally when she trembled in his arms, he lifted her and carried her across to his bed. For a long moment, he stood at the side of the bed and gazed down at her. Her beauty was remarkable, and a tender ache filled his chest. The unfamiliar feeling tugged at him and Sébastien let the warmth spread through his blood. Madeleine's hair fanned out on the pillow around her head and her eyes had taken on a dark and mysterious haze; her lips were dark, red and inviting him to return. As he watched, she unlaced the silken red chemise and slipped it over her head.

Ah, God. Her nipples were a dusky pink and erect. His gaze lingered on the pale skin of her breasts. They were like alabaster, pure and untouched. Slowly he reached down and cupped each of her breasts in his hand, and they were warm beneath his fingers. A groan tore from his throat as a tremble ran through his body. Slowly and gently, Sébastien ran his hands lower and untied the laces she had fashioned at the side of the black skirt and slipped it down over her feet.

She wore nothing beneath it and he held his breath, fighting his own need, determined to pleasure her before giving in to his own pressing desire. He lay beside her and her hands touched his shoulders, lingering on his chest and moving down to his manhood. He grasped her fingers before she could touch him again, fighting the greed that threatened to overwhelm him.

"Slowly. I will pleasure you slowly." He lifted his head and held her gaze. Her eyes drew him in deeply, inviting him to take her, but he smiled and shook his head. "So sweet, so beautiful."

He lowered his hand to the curls between her legs and cupped her sex, and her body bucked beneath his fingers. Slowly he searched for the hard nub and smiled at her as he found it. Her eyes were wide, and her lips were open with wonder. Gently, he circled around it, teasing her and lightly brushing his hand in the fine silken hair that covered her.

She shuddered beneath him each time his fingers brushed her. She pushed her hips higher.

"Please don't stop. I need more." Her voice was ragged, and he lowered his head and laved her nipple at the same time as his finger entered her hot, damp folds.

Her scream surprised him as he drew her nipple into his mouth and sucked. She shuddered beneath him.

***

Madeleine was floating above the soft feather mattress as the last of the exquisite tremors rippled through her. Sébastien had moved up beside her and whispered soft endearments softly as his lips grazed her neck. Gentle caresses warmed her as his fingers continued to explore her body. Sweet sensation such as she had never imagined.

What new passions will my lover find me today? What pleasures unheard of, undreamed of? Now, for the first time, she understood the words Aunt Josephine had written in her diary. Slowly, Sébastien lifted her until his arms were around her and his hard body was pressed along her length. In one swift roll he was on top of her and he lowered his head and took her mouth. He used his tongue to lightly open her lips and as he thrust it firmly between them, he moved one hand between them and plunged his fingers inside her. She could not get enough of the feel of his fingers touching her, stretching her and she waited, knowing he was preparing her.

"I am afraid of hurting you." His words hummed against her lips as the tip of his hot manhood pressed against her, replacing his gentle fingers. She smiled as he murmured what was going to happen, sweet promises of how he would take her to heaven and back.

"I am all right." Madeleine could not help but smile at his gentle words.

Cherished. He made her feel cherished and protected. It had been many months since anyone had cared for her well-being, but no one had ever cared for her like this. He was not the pirate who had frightened her days ago. This was a man who was slowly and lovingly showing her the magic of her body, and the magic that could be created between them. He knew where to touch her and to kiss her softly, so she craved more. He knew how to make her quiver as she waited for him to take her. Her body was humming with anticipation as Sébastien lifted her and her breath quickened.

A slight sting, a stretching until she was gloriously full and a shaft of pleasure so intense struck her that she forgot about the brief discomfort. She gasped, and he took his mouth with hers. Madeleine's senses were heightened as each new feeling built on the next exquisite wave of pleasure until she again reached the sweet crest his gentle fingers had taken her to. This time the pleasure was more complete as he filled her, and slowly withdrew, teasing her with his heat at her core. Her body showed her how to move with him, move for move, kiss for kiss, and shared looks that were as pleasurable as the sensations rocking her body.

Sébastien held her gaze as he slipped deeper into her, all the while whispering endearments.

"You are so beautiful."

His reverent whisper washed over her and the throbbing between her thighs built almost unbearably as his hips pushed against hers and instinctively she opened her legs wider. Light flashed against her vision and she closed her eyes as the pleasure peaked and held as he moved inside her.

With a guttural cry, he thrust once more, and Madeleine trembled as his brown eyes darkened with pleasure. Sébastien dropped his head to her shoulder and she reached down and touched his chest where she could feel the beating of his heart against her breast.

Rolling her, he took her in his arms, and Madeleine rested her head on his shoulder. The last thing she was aware of before she fell asleep was the feel of his hand gently stroking her hair as he held her close.

Chapter Eighteen

"Tell me more about the islands." Madeleine lifted her head from Sébastien's chest and he ran his fingers through her hair. They were only half a day's sailing from New Orleans and he had left the wheelhouse three hours ago to come down and check on her. As they had done for the past four days and nights, they had ended up in his bed. There had been no further problems with the crew, and he and Mr. Abrahams had kept a close eye on the new men. They had worked as hard as the rest of the crew and had given him no problem, but he would pay them off once they docked.

A shaft of sunlight shone through the aperture in the hull and bathed Madeleine's head in a soft light. Her green eyes were wide and fixed on him and as he watched, she trailed a finger down his chest, and would have continued further down had he not captured her fingers in his.

"I must go up and let Mr. Abrahams have some rest. I have turned you into a wanton, madam." He pulled her hand to his mouth and kissed her fingers. She laughed softly and slid up in the bed alongside him until her soft breasts pressed against his chest.

Sébastien groaned. "I must go above deck."

"Just five more minutes…please? It is lonely down here without you." Madeleine had only gone above deck once a day on this return journey, to keep her out of the sight of the suspect crewmen. And each time she had been in Sébastien's company. If the crew had previously doubted that she was his woman, they had no doubt of it now. He had held her tightly as they watched the sun set each night and she had clung to him.

"Tell me again about the island you are going to live on." Her warm lips nuzzled into his neck and he was lost.

Sébastien pushed her away gently and rolled over to the edge of the bed. "I will tell you if you stay over there where you cannot tempt me, wench." He grinned at her as he propped himself up on one elbow, marvelling at the confidence she had discovered in her body since he had introduced her to the world of pleasure between a man and a woman.

Was it only four days ago? She had bewitched him. Never before had he experienced the need for a woman such as she had raised in him. Last night he had lain beside her, listening to her soft breathing, her hand curled safely in his. He could not let Madeleine go. That realization had hit him like a thunderbolt from the storm that had woken him as it roared above the vessel. He would try to persuade her to come to the islands with him. If he could not persuade her, he would accompany her back to Bellerose, although the thought of delaying his trip to the Hawaiian Islands was not attractive to him.

"There are many islands, but the last time I visited I chose the land which I shall purchase. I will have the best sugar plantation in the islands and it will be worked by free men." His breath caught in his throat as she lowered her hand enticingly and brushed it through the auburn curls nestled between her thighs.

"I shall marry, and I shall raise a family." His mouth dried as he watched her fingers move slowly in a circle before she slipped one finger lower. "Perhaps I can find a suitable wife before I leave. Do you know of any woman who may like to marry an old pirate, Madeleine?"

He lifted his gaze and her eyes were wide

as she raised both of her hands to her mouth.

"What are you asking, Sébastien?" Her voice was husky.

"What do you think?" He sat up and put his hands behind his head as he watched her. If he did not restrain his hands, he would not be able to resist touching her and he must go above deck sooner than later. "Give it some thought as we wait for the tide to take us up the river."

Madeleine was quiet and he wondered if he had spoken too soon.

"Before I can suggest a suitable woman for your needs"—she shot him a sultry smile—"I would have to think more of my quest to find Great Aunt Josephine's necklace."

"Josephine?" He narrowed his eyes as he realised what she had said. "Was your great aunt Josephine du Bois?"

Madeleine sat up and moved over beside him, her expression alight with interest. "Yes, why do you ask? Did you know of her?"

"Yes, I knew her briefly." He wondered how much Madeleine knew of her great aunt's story. There had been quite a scandal when she had taken up with the Russian fur trader. Sébastien had not been long in New Orleans when he had met Josephine at a soiree at the governor's residence. After that he had attended a few receptions at the du Bois house. He did not want to tell Madeleine too much; he would have to give some thought to what he said. Swinging his legs over the side of the bed, he reached for his breeches.

Madeleine's eyes were bright, and she smiled. "I cannot believe that you have met my Great Aunt Josephine. I met her once when I was a small child when she and her husband, Uncle Francois visited us at Bellerose Hall. Her eyes clouded as she mentioned her home. Sébastien had been pleased to see her laugh and smile often over the past four days.

He reached for his shirt and pulled it over his head. They would talk of her great aunt later. "I will be above deck until we navigate the turn of the tide and dock safely at the wharf. "Ensure you lock the door while I am gone, and don't open it to anybody." He leaned over and put his hands either side of her and satisfaction warmed his chest as she raised her lips to his.

"Stay safe. We shall be in New Orleans by nightfall." Reluctantly Sébastien left her and crossed to the door and waited. "Come and draw the bolt while I am still outside the door. And ensure you open the door to no one."

Madeleine slid from the bed and Sébastien shook his head as he watched her walk across the carpeted floor. She was not self-conscious in her nakedness and her thick red hair fell to her waist as she walked slowly toward him. Her breasts bobbed gently as she crossed the room and his eyes were drawn to the dusky pink nipples. He tried to put a stern look on his face but knew he failed miserably as a grin tugged at his mouth.

"You are a wanton wench, my dear." He pulled her into his arms and pressed his mouth to hers. "But I still want you to give serious thought to my question." He lifted his head and stared at her. "Will you promise me you will consider coming with me."

"Why would you ask me to come with you?" Her eyes were wide and despite her nakedness, they were guileless. She truly had no idea of what he felt for her.

"Because, my love, I cannot imagine my life without you beside me." He stared at her. "I know it has not been a long time, but I have fallen in love with you, Madeleine. Think about that while I am gone."

A small gasp escaped her lips and as she pressed against him, her mouth was warm against his neck. She stood there for a moment and her body trembled against his. When she pulled away her face was wet with tears. "I will give it some deep thought, I promise."

Sébastien lifted his thumb and gently

wiped her tears away. "Happy tears, I hope?"

"Happy tears." Madeleine nodded and smiled sweetly at him. "Now go and see to your boat, Captain. I am going to have a wash and try to repair my clothing so I can walk the streets of New Orleans as a lady."

"As soon as we dock, I have to make a brief visit to the town. I will only be gone a short while, but I will come back down to dress before I go ashore." Sébastien wanted to get this task over quickly, collect his payment from the governor and then focus on Madeleine. "Get some sleep. When I return we shall leave the *Maiden* together and find some lodgings in the town."

He looked around and spoke quietly. "And then I shall leave this life behind. Shall we do it together? Think on that, Madeleine."

Sébastien waited in the passageway until he heard the snick of the bolt on the other side of the door.

***

Madeleine leaned against the door and closed her eyes. Her life had changed so much over the past weeks. Was it too soon to make a life changing decision—forgo her quest and move to the islands that Sébastien spoke of? Was it selfish to think of her needs...or had she been thinking of her needs all along? The past four days in Sébastien's bed had brought her truly to adulthood and now she had to think of what she must do.

It was an impossible choice to make. In her heart, she knew it would be very easy to follow this man to the ends of the earth. But what would she do about Bellerose Hall and the necklace? She could not give up on her promise to restore the estate.

When Sébastien had called her, 'my love', the emotion that had filled her had been as satisfying as the heights to which he had taken her in his bed over the past days. Madeleine shivered and hugged herself, looking down at her breasts and bare legs in disbelief. She was naked in her pirate's cabin and she was smiling. Had she changed so much she could forgo her quest?

No, I must complete it.

Confusion filled her as she slipped into the curtained alcove and poured the water from the pitcher to the bowl. The light was fading, and Madeleine squinted into the looking glass that was propped on the cupboard. Never did she remember her lips being so red and plump and she brushed at a small red mark on her neck where Sébastien's beard had scraped her white skin.

She had experienced many new feelings in

these few weeks on the *Maiden*. Should I not let them take over my thoughts? Perhaps Sébastien would tire of her when he had satisfied himself in her body? The first glimmers of doubt began to pierce her euphoria. She was inexperienced in the relationships between a man and a woman.

Did he really mean what he said? Am I his love? Perhaps she should take some time to consider her own feelings. To get back to shore and see if he stays true to me? Madeleine had no doubt that her feelings for Sébastien were steadfast but could she risk being left alone...once more in her life?

Why would a man like Sébastien truly be interested in a young inexperienced woman such as I?

She could not accept his proposal. She would seek Great Aunt Josephine's necklace, she would sell it and send the proceeds home to Bellerose Hall so it could be restored. Mayhap then she could consider Sébastien's proposal...if it still stood.

She had promised she would find the necklace. Although the promise was more to myself than to anyone else.

Perhaps Sébastien would change his mind and help her? Once he realised she was determined to find the necklace? He had not elaborated about how he knew Josephine and another niggle of doubt snaked through Madeleine's mind. He had displayed scant interest in the necklace, yet when he had recognised Aunt Josephine's name he had not really been forthcoming about his knowledge of her. Did he know more than he was telling?

Why, oh why, do I doubt him?

Dismissing the thoughts from her mind, Madeleine lifted a handful of clothes from the chest and proceeded to look for something befitting a lady to wear into New Orleans.

Some time later, a light tap at the door interrupted her as she braided her hair. She had found a modest dress and was awaiting Sébastien's return. When he came back from the governor's, she would put her slippers on. Her meagre possessions which had been in her reticule and sewn into her black dress were now safely wrapped in a woollen shawl she had found at the bottom of the chest. Crossing to the door, she went to unbolt the latch and then she remembered his warning.

Do not open the door for anyone.

"Who's there?" she called softly.

"It's Cook. I have some food for you. The captain said you may be hungry, miss."

Madeleine reached for the latch and hesitated. The man's voice sounded different to the cook that Sébastien had called Crawford. "What do you have for me?"

She wanted to hear him speak again so she could be sure. "Ah…there is some—"

Goose bumps rose on Madeleine's arms as she heard a scuffle and whispering from the other side of the door.

"Some soup, miss."

"Thank you, I'm not hungry. Perhaps you could take it up to the captain?" Unease snaked through her.

"I will just bring it in for the captain when he comes down."

"No, thank you."

A loud curse reached her, and she watched as the wooden handle lowered until it reached the bolt she had drawn on the cabin side of the door. Madeleine stepped back with her hands over her mouth, looking around for somewhere to hide, before she realised they could not get in. She hurried over to the table and picked up the heavy chair and dragged it across to the door to be doubly sure.

She stood there for a few moments until all was quiet. Walking over to the bed she sat down and put her hands over her face. The fear that had filled her the other day when the man had hurt Jake and had grabbed her had returned. Now that they were close to New

Orleans, she was unsafe. She had the knowledge of the necklace and where it perhaps was hidden but finding it may not be an easy task.

Safe at rest, at home.

She would have to trust Sébastien and together they would search. Then she would make her mind up about her future and what course of action she would take.

Chapter Nineteen

Luck was with the *Maiden* as they sailed in on the incoming tide and the docking at the wharf was speedy and trouble free. By sunset, the sails were down and there was much jovial calling out to each other among the crew who were looking forward to going ashore. As they manouvered the boat into position against the wooden quay, Sébastien put his hand to his eyes and searched along the river's edge. There was no sign of the British frigate that had brought Madeleine across the ocean. He wondered whether her uncle had left New Orleans.

He rolled his shoulders and stretched. To have this final mission behind him was a great relief. The crew was tired and as ready to spend some time on the land as he was. He grinned; he knew his tiredness had more to do with the return journey and Madeleine being in his bed, rather than the intercept itself, which had gone more smoothly than any other mission he had led. At the outset, he had worried about Madeleine's presence on board, but it seemed she had brought him luck. The assault by the crewman had been more problematic for the voyage than the intercept itself.

"You look tired, Captain." His first mate came to stand beside him. "Are you going ashore tonight?"

"Yes, I will escort Captain Lamoreau to the governor as soon as we are secure." The French captain had been compliant and had caused no trouble aboard the vessel as they had travelled back. "Why do you ask?" The gangplank had been lowered but the crew was still securing ropes to the quay.

It was out of character for Mr. Abrahams to ask Sébastien of his business unless it was to do with the *Maiden*, which would now be under his command.

"The three new crewmen have left the boat and gone ashore already. They must have jumped to the quay before we turned the bow in."

"Three?"

"The man who was secured has gone too. I went down to check on him when I noticed the other two had gone but they must have released him. They have all gone. They must have chosen a time when I was occupied below."

Sébastien frowned. He was concerned about Madeleine's assailant being on the loose.

"Can you keep a close watch on who comes on board while I am with the governor?"

Mr. Abrahams nodded and Sébastien turned for the ladder. "I will be as quick as I can in town." He looked back over his shoulder. "Where is young Jake?" The boy was usually hovering around the first mate and was nowhere in sight.

Mr. Abrahams frowned. "I'm not sure. He must have gone below."

Unease filled Sébastien as he climbed down the ladder. He walked along the dark passageway and entered the small cabin where the man had been locked up. The door was open and the ropes which had bound him had been cut and were lying on the wooden floor. Stepping back into the passageway he looked around, checking in each of the other spaces as he passed them. It had been a mistake hiring them for the voyage, but he hoped they were long gone by now.

He tapped lightly on the cabin door. "Madeleine, it's me. Sébastien."

The bolt unlatched with a sharp creak and the door opened slowly. The wanton of a couple of hours ago had been replaced by a young lady in a modest dress, her hair braided and coiled neatly at the nape of her neck. Madeleine stood demurely in the shadows watching him.

"You look very pretty."

She bobbed a curtsy, holding her skirts wide. "Thank you, Captain."

Sébastien reached for her and pulled her to him. "I missed you."

Although her arms circled his waist, there was a slight distance in her response and he looked down at her. "Is everything all right?"

Relief filled him as she turned her cheek into his shoulder.

"I was frightened when you were ashore. Someone tried to get into the cabin."

"Who tried? Did they harm you?"

"I don't know, and no, I was not harmed." Madeleine tipped her head back slowly. "And now, I am a little sad our journey has ended. I will be honest with you. I am unsure of what to do."

Sébastien's heart sank and he forgot about the intruders who had tried to get into he cabin. Perhaps she had made her decision already and was not going to accept his proposal. "To do?"

"Part of it is about Great Aunt Josephine's necklace." A measure of relief ran though him but he would take this slowly. "What concerns you?"

"I have been selfish."

Tears filled her eyes and threatened to spill

over. He lifted his hand and cradled her cheek. "I think you have been very brave."

She shook her head and pulled away from him. "No. Every decision I have made has been for me."

"Every decision you have made has been for your well-being and safety. From what I have seen of your actions and heard of your thoughts, your motives have been selfless."

"Sébastien, I know that you think I am foolish." Her harsh cry tugged at him as she pulled away from his hold, but he let her go and she began to pace the cabin. "I have not given this enough thought. Even if I find the necklace I cannot do what I intended. Bellerose Hall is in the hands of Uncle Titus." She turned and walked back toward him, her hands clasped in front of her chest, her brow wrinkled and her lips in a straight line. "And how would I get the necklace or the money to England? There is no one I can send it to."

She stopped pacing when she reached him. "It was a foolish hope that I could change anything at Bellerose Hall. Jake had more understanding than I did, and his words made me think."

"Jake's words? What did he say?" Sébastien reached out and took her hand in his.

"He told me that having servants is very

much like the slavery that you fight against." She shook her head. "Oh, I know it is different in many ways, but it made me ponder. I cannot change the way things are and they were the foolish, immature thoughts of a silly young girl to think that I could."

"No, not foolish. Noble and brave." He reached his other hand up and gently lifted her chin, but her tears continued.

"And why would you want me to accompany you to your new life? Can I believe that you will not leave me?"

Sébastien cradled Madeleine's face between his hands and stared into her eyes trying to convey what he was feeling through his touch before he spoke.

"I called you my love before, but perhaps I did not put it clearly enough." Her eyes widened as he held her gaze. "I love you, Madeleine, and it would break my heart if you chose not to come with me. But if you wish, I will help you find the necklace and take it back to England before you accompany me"

"You would?" Her voice calmed and Sébastien's heart stilled as he looked into the emerald depths of her eyes.

"I would, Madeleine."

"Oh Sébastien." She lifted one hand and placed it gently on his cheek before she stretched up on her toes and laced her arms around his neck. Her breath was a whisper on his lips as she pulled his head down. "I will follow you."

Her lips were warm and pliant beneath his, and Sébastien closed his eyes as he gathered her close and held her to him. They stood quietly together, and it was as though, in that moment, they made a vow. Finally, he lifted his head and regarded her, his heart thudding so hard he was sure she would feel it through her dress.

"We will talk some more when we go ashore together." Madeleine opened her mouth, but he put a finger on her lips.

"Not now. We shall talk later. There is much you don't know. Now I must leave you very briefly."

"Can I come with you now?"

"No. I must go alone. Keep the door latched securely and pack your things ready to leave when I return. Do not open it to a soul." He kept his voice soft as he dropped his head for a final swift kiss. The sooner he left, the sooner he would be back and their life together would begin. "Don't forget to pack your other dress. I have become quite enamoured of that scanty outfit. I would hate for you to leave it on board."

Madeleine's laugh followed him as he pulled the door closed behind him.

***

Sébastien paced up and down the narrow hallway behind the ballroom of La Salle Conde Theatre, his footsteps echoing in the narrow space. He had been waiting for Carondelet for more than three hours, and an hour ago the governor's aide had come to him to advise that he would be the next to see the governor who was attending a quadroon Carnival ball at the theatre. The French captain waited quietly in a chair beside the door and seemed disinclined to move. At first, the governor had refused to see Sébastien and he suspected that the long wait was deliberate, due to his insistence on seeing Carondelet tonight. He had attended these balls himself and knew that the dancing could go until dawn. He turned and paced one more length of the corridor considering whether to go back to the *Maiden*.

"Can I get you a brandy, Captain?" The aide flicked the Frenchman a scathing glance, yet he did not appear at all concerned about the long wait Sébastien had endured. There was nothing to be gained by losing his temper. "Thank you, but no." The aide clicked his heels and left the room. Sebastien stood and prowled around the room looking at the portraits that covered the walls.

"Holy Mother." Sébastien peered at the portrait in front of him just as the door opened to admit the governor and the aide. Josephine du Bois looked down at him, her expression serious, but capturing his attention was the glittering emerald diamond necklace that covered the bare expanse of Josephine's chest above her ball gown. More than twenty square-cut and oval emeralds were nestled between a myriad of countless diamonds. The artist had captured the light perfectly and the glittering gems were the focus of the portrait. He must bring Madeline to see this in the morning. She would be excited to see the necklace did exist.

"Good evening, Captain."

Sébastien reluctantly tore his gaze from the portrait and the object of Madeleine's quest. It would be worth a king's ransom. No wonder Jean-Luc was seeking information.

The governor looked at the French captain and a smile of satisfaction crossed his face.

"Governor." Sebastien inclined his head as a mark of respect.

"Did you know the necklace in that portrait has never been found? It is widely assumed that it was destroyed in the fire that killed Josephine. What is your interest in it, Captain?"

"I have no interest. I had not seen it before

and I was observing the portrait only a moment before you came in."

The governor gave him a curious look before he nodded and reached into the leather pouch that the aide handed to him.

"And now to business, Captain."

***

There was little packing for Madeleine to do. She slid her bare feet into her beribboned slippers and lit the lamp on the table before laying the shawl on the bed. She held up the red and black outfit that she had fashioned to wear on the ship and smiled. She had not thought to take it with her but now she placed it on the shawl with her ribbons before rolling it up in a neat bundle. Placing it on the bed beside her, she looked around the cabin which had been her home for the past weeks.

Her doubts had been dispelled with Sébastien's words and a warm flush ran through her as she held his declaration of love in her thoughts. She wondered what was so urgent that he had had to leave her.

All will be well. She looked forward to embarking on a new adventure; this time with Sébastien by her side.

###

Madeleine was asleep by the time Sébastien returned. She woke briefly as he climbed into the bed and wrapped his arms around her and whispered into her hair.

"A successful visit, my love. And I have something to show you in the morning that will make you very happy."

Madeleine rolled over and pressed against Sébastien's naked length and whispered saucily. "You can show me now if you would like to."

His deep laugh vibrated on her chest and she placed her hand on him. He was ready as he had been each time they were in bed together—and other times that they weren't and had made use of other alcoves in the cabin to slake their desire for each other. Madeline sighed with pleasure as her fingers stroked his silken but firm length.

His voice was husky as he lifted her hand away. "Now that you are awake, let me tell you what I have found."

"Can it wait?" she murmured as her lips found his neck.

"I have found the necklace you seek." He grinned as Madeleine sat bolt upright in the bed.

"The necklace? Great Aunt Josephine's necklace?"

He nodded with a smile and she threw her arms around his neck. "Oh, Sébastien, where is it?"

"Be calm, my love. I will show you in the morning. I have found a portrait of your aunt wearing the necklace." He buried his face in her hair and she smiled. If the necklace was found, perhaps she could sell it and somehow send the money to Bellerose and she could follow Sébastien's dreams?

"As soon as we awake, I shall take you and show you. We shall then book a passage for England as I believe there is a three week wait, so time is of the essence."

Madeleine's happiness was complete. It was the first time since her family had been killed that she felt free and happy. If indeed, they found the actual necklace in the next few weeks, she would give deep thought to her future. She must have stiffened in his grasp as he dropped his head and ran a soft kiss along her cheek.

"What is it?"

"You read me so well." Madeleine turned her face to meet his lips. "I just need to be sure of what I will do."

Sébastien lifted his head and stared at her, his dark eyes shining in the soft moonlight. "You are the only one who can make that decision. If you have any doubt, you must think long and hard."

Madeleine swallowed her doubt and smiled up at him as her fingers found their quarry. "Speaking of long and hard…"

It was a long time before they slept.

Chapter Twenty

Madeleine's anticipation at seeing the necklace and the portrait of her Great Aunt Josephine was satisfying to watch. Her belief in the existence of the necklace had been confirmed and she drew in an excited breath as she grasped Sébastien's hand.

"Can we go and seek it now?"

Sébastien had not shared with Madeleine his knowledge that Josephine's house had burned to the ground. It was not the right time to deflate her excitement. He would take her to the land where the house had once stood and perhaps they would find a clue of what may have happened to the precious necklace. He would get Madeleine to tell him what she knew and together they would search.

Despite his joy in her excitement, a heavy feeling settled in Sébastien's stomach as the time came closer to booking their passage to England. His dream of starting anew and moving to the islands was slowly dissipating like the morning mist over the Mississippi river and he was beginning to wonder if he had made too hasty a decision. When he was in Madeleine's presence, and particularly when her hands and mouth were on him, he had no doubt that he wanted to be with her. When he was alone, the doubts crept in and he struggled to make sense of the joy he took in being with her and the need to accompany her to fulfil her quest...which would put his own dreams in jeopardy.

"Mr. Abrahams has told me of a ship that is departing for England next week but the berths are filling quickly." Sébastien said as he opened the cabin door. He shook his head with a smile. "Still abed, you lazy strumpet?"

Madeleine slid her long bare legs over the side of the bed and her dainty feet rested on the carpet. The now familiar jerk of desire ran through his blood and Sébastien pushed it aside.

"I shall go into town and book our berths while you prepare yourself to go ashore to see the portrait."

"I can be ready quickly." She smiled up at him.

"No need. I will simply be standing in a crowd for a long while. There is a great demand for berths because there is a shortage. The information came to Mr. Abrahams and I must go quickly."

"Sebastien?" Madeline chewed her lip and frowned at him. A shaft of worry shot through him and he wondered if she had changed her mind.

"Yes? What is it?"

"When you are ashore, would you…would you see if there is any sign of my uncle?"

Sébastien chastised himself silently as the guilt of taking Madeleine's innocence came hurtling back. He had forgotten about her uncle entirely since he'd noticed the frigate had departed. The pleasures of her body had addled his brain. Perhaps the decisions he had made were equally as foolish?

He nodded. "I will." He cast a long glance at her and tried to ignore the bewitching pull she had over him, and his voice sounded terse even to his own ears. "Ready yourself and we shall go to the salon to see the portrait as soon as I return."

Her wide smile, her beauty, her innocence all presented a picture that caused great confusion in him. Sébastien forced a smile to his face and turned quickly and closed the door behind him. He would consider his actions on his way to book the berths…or one single berth for Madeleine. He had some serious thinking to do.

***

Madeleine took time to wash and dress herself suitably to travel into town. She managed to put together an outfit that bespoke of a lady...of sorts. She waited in the cabin for Sébastien to return. It had been almost midday when he had left and now he had been gone for hours. She began to worry about his safety...and then she began to worry that he had changed his mind. Foolish thoughts. If he had changed his mind about her, he would not abandon her on his boat.

Perhaps he had found Uncle Titus?

Even worse, perhaps he had gone to look for the necklace by himself. She paced the cabin, her hard-soled slippers clicking on the wooden floor each time she stepped off the square of carpet.

The light faded as night fell and the lamp cast soft shadows around the cabin. Sébastien had been almost the whole day and Madeleine prayed he would return soon. Her worry dissolved, and impatience filled her as she wandered around the cabin, picking up unfamiliar instruments and examining them. She was ready to leave with him as soon as he returned. Another hour passed, and she walked to the aperture in the hull and looked out. She tapped her fingers against the timber as the glimmers of doubt came back.

What if he doesn't come back? What if he just leaves me here?

All was dark and quiet on the quay, and there was no sign of any movement on the wharf. If it had been like that the night she had escaped Uncle Titus, her life would be very different now. A tap sounded at the door and Madeleine ran lightly across the cabin as relief filled her. Her doubts had been unnecessary. He wouldn't leave her. "Sébastien?"

"No, Miss Madeleine. It is Jake. I came to say goodbye before I leave."

Disappointment was like a stone in her stomach. "Where are you going?"

There was a hesitation and then Jake's voice came through the door. "I have found...a better vessel."

Madeleine was surprised as she had understood him to be happy on the *Maiden* and had assumed that he would continue on the vessel when Mr. Abrahams took over as captain.

"I am leaving now, so can I...come in...to say goodbye?" His voice was shaking. "Or maybe you can come out?"

Madeleine frowned as she unlatched the

door. Jake sounded upset and he had been a true friend to her. She pulled the door open slowly but the young boy did not enter.

"It's all right to come in, Jake. The captain is not here."

"And isn't that unfortunate for you." She gasped as the door was flung wide open and two men pushed past her before grabbing her arms roughly.

"Oh miss, I am so sorry. They made me do it." Tears rolled down Jake's face from eyes which were wide with fear.

The crew man who had assaulted her had his arm curled around Jake's neck and a knife against his throat.

"It's all right, Jake." An icy calm descended on Madeleine as she reassured him. She did not want to move for fear the knife at his throat slipped.

"Shall I slit his throat in front of you, madam?" The man she knew as Dirk pushed Jake in through the door and she turned her head to watch them enter. "Or shall we wait for the captain to return and kill you both together?"

Madeleine held herself rigid and tried to catch Jake's eye, but the young boy had dropped his head. She opened her mouth but the man to her left put his filthy hand on her lips. For a moment she was tempted to bite his fingers but realised she must be compliant if Jake's life was to be spared.

She shook her head and he lifted his hand.

"I will not scream. What is it you want from me?" While ever the knife was at Jake's throat she would do as they asked, no matter what.

She prayed that Sébastien would return, and then in the next thought, she hoped he would not. There was too much danger and the space they were in was too confined and there was no one nearby to help. If they had been up on the deck there would be more of a chance of getting away.

"You will come with us and lead us to the treasure you told the boy about." The man's voice deepened with suspicion. "Or has the pirate gone to get it already?"

Jake squealed as the sailor pressed the knife against his neck and Madeleine watched with horrified fascination as a trickle of blood ran down the blade.

"No! No, leave him be or I will tell you nothing. The captain has gone ashore for a short time."

Two of the men exchanged a look. "I would wager he will return with his pockets full of gold. This night gets better as each minute passes."

"Come, we are wasting time. We will come back for his gold after she leads us to the necklace." His cold eyes flicked a glance toward her and she shivered at the intent in his eyes. She wondered what her fate was to be.

Rough hands dragged her through the door and she looked around in panic, wondering if she would ever see Jake and Sébastien again. But one of her fears was allayed.

"The boy will come with us. It will be good leverage to get the wench to talk." He pushed Jake ahead of him toward the door, the knife still glinting in the lamplight.

One of the other men was ahead of her and the other followed as Madeleine climbed the ladder to the deck. It was dark and only a faint light shone from the wheelhouse. She scanned around the deck without moving her head, trying to find the first mate, but there was no sign of anyone.

"You are clever for a wench, that is for certain." The voice coming from behind her turned Madeleine's stomach to water. "Are you clever enough not to call for help?" She turned and lifted her hand as his spittle hit her face.

"Do you want your young friend to stay alive? What say you, wench? Do we need to gag you?" His voice was loud, and she prayed someone would hear and come see what was happening. But all was still.

"No." She shook her head and they pulled her to the gangplank, with Jake close behind. Stepping onto land for the first time in three weeks, Madeleine's legs trembled as her feet hit the hard road and she fought to keep her balance.

The man with the knife gestured to the man on her left and he let her go briefly as they swapped positions. There was nothing she could do as the knife was once again at Jake's neck.

Putrid breath fanned her face as Dirk leaned in to her. "Now, you will tell us where this treasure can be found."

Madeleine thought quickly. If Jake was to be spared and Sébastien kept safe, she would lead them to Aunt Josephine's house.

"I have not been there and do not know the house, but I can tell you where it is."

"Then tell us." He pushed his face into hers and she recoiled with distaste.

"Ah, she thinks she is better than us because she has been in the captain's bed. Well, wench, watch how quickly he and his brother rid themselves of you when you no longer have the treasure they seek." Dirk's voice was hard yet full of amused satisfaction

His brother? What did Sébastien's brother have to do with this? Fear crawled into Madeleine's throat as all her doubts came rushing back. One of the final things Sébastien had mentioned as he had left her had been the necklace. Was that all he sought from her?

"You thought it was your pretty charms?" Dirk laughed, and a shiver ran down Madeleine's back. "It wasn't. Nor the booty between your legs."

No. She straightened her back. I will not lose faith. This man knows nothing.

A grimy hand grabbed her chin and turned her face to his. A mouth with black-stained teeth hovered near her lips as the man lowered his face closer to hers. His fingers pressed into her cheeks and she bit back a cry of pain.

"So where are we going to?" he said. "Where is this treasure hidden?"

"The necklace is in my great aunt's house. But I do not know who lives there since she died."

"Where is this house?"

Madeleine closed her eyes remembering the inscription in the front of the diary that was imprinted in her mind. "It is in Rue Toulouse next to a cemetery…but I don't even know where that is."

"Good. We will find it. Now, you will look

like a whore who is out for an evening stroll with some lonely sailors. If you call for help or try to escape, the boy will die." His fingers squeezed her arm so hard she bit her lip to stop the cry of pain escaping her lips. "Do you understand me?"

Madeleine dropped her head and whispered. "I understand you." If she could delay them, perhaps Sébastien or some of the crew would return. There was no point trying to escape or she would be responsible for Jake's death. All she could pray for was that if she told these men what she knew that they would be able to find the necklace. They must have looked like a strange group but as they walked through the streets no one cast them a second glance.

It was strange to be walking on land. Madeleine looked at the mysterious alleys, covered passageways, two story houses with ornate lacework and narrow streets laid out in a square grid. Even though it was late in the evening, the streets were crowded with men and women in evening dress who paid scant attention to four people keeping to the shadows. Snatches of unfamiliar languages floated by and there was much laughter. She kept her head down as they walked until the men came to a stop outside a tavern.

"Wait here. I'm going into the tavern to find out where this Rue Toulouse is." Dirk jerked his head toward her. "What is your aunt's name?"

"Du Bois." Madeleine said. "It was du Bois."

"Make sure you watch them." His whisper was harsh and the way he looked at her sent a shiver down her back. If they found the necklace, she feared for Jake's and her own safety. If they went back to the *Maiden*, she feared they would hurt Sébastien, too. Her mind flitted from one thought to another and she fought the helpless panic rising in her throat.

The two men spoke quietly and peered into the tavern. Madeleine was surprised that the sailors did not know where to find the street she had named. Although she had expected New Orleans to be smaller and more uncivilized, she was surprised by the number of people in the streets; although it was still not as big as the English towns she was used to.

Shadows flickered on the wall backlit by the street lamps as they waited in the dark beneath an overhanging porch. The sweet smell of the burning oil was cloying and Madeleine swallowed as bile rose up and burned her throat. It was a combination of the smell and the fear for their fate once they reached the house. The outcome of the search for the necklace was probably inconsequential; she did not doubt that these men would kill them. Looking up from beneath her lashes she caught Jake's eye. His eyes were wide, and he was trying to tell her something. He inclined his head toward the fence at the end of the porch, just behind where he was standing. He mouthed words to her and she stared at him trying to see what he was saying before looking across at the fence. There was a small gap in the planks at the base, and she realised Jake's intention as he whispered softly.

"I'll bring help."

The two men still had their heads together and Madeleine strained to hear their words, but their thick accents made their words difficult to understand. She stepped closer so that she would partially block their view of Jake. As she moved, Jake dropped to the ground and rolled through the small hole. Before they were aware of him moving, he was through the gap and the darkness swallowed him.

For a moment, the weight lifted a little from Madeleine's heart. If only Jake could find Sébastien…

"Oy!" the man closest to her turned around and the look on his face was almost comical as he realised Jake was gone. "Where the dickens did the little bugger go?"

Madeleine put her hands to her face and shook her head, pretending she hadn't seen him. The stocky sailor grabbed her arm and his filthy breath hit her before he turned to the man with the strong accent. "You go and find him. He can't have got far. I'll hold her. Quickly, before Dirk comes back out."

Madeleine closed her eyes. How many more men did they have helping them?

Before he could go, the door opened, and Dirk swaggered out. "We're almost there. Rue Toulouse is only two streets away. Come..." He looked around and his eyes narrowed. "Fuck. Where's the boy? Don't tell me you buffoons let him escape?" He stared at Madeleine and his voice was harsh with the same anger that fired his eyes. He reached out and squeezed her arm and the pain shot up to her shoulder. "You may think he has gone to your pirate, but he'll get no help from that quarter."

She twisted in his grasp as the pressure of his fingers became unbearable and she shivered at the malice in his voice.

"The tattle in the tavern was all about the mysterious necklace. Jean-Luc Leclerc has been waiting impatiently for his brother's return." A smile split his face, but it was not pleasant. "The word is around that the fur trader, Lutchenko gave a Russian heirloom to his mistress—" his fingers squeezed harder "—but no one knows who the woman was, so overhearing your talk to your little friend was a windfall for me."

She let out her breath as his fingers loosened on her arm and he turned to the other two men. "Forget the boy, we have to work quickly. We're the only ones who know the name of the mistress."

Madeleine shrunk back into the shadows away from his intent gaze as his eyes narrowed.

"Or are we? Does the pirate know who Lutchenko's woman was?" He shook her arm. "Did you tell him where she lived? Does he know where the treasure is?"

"No, I did not." She shook her head; she could at least answer half of his question truthfully and prayed he would not question her further. The other two men stepped in close to her side, and Dirk strode ahead and led the way, keeping to the shadows of the porches that overhung the narrow footpath. Occasionally they passed a tavern where light spilled out onto the road. For the time being, Madeleine cooperated; she really had no other option, but she kept alert and scanned the street ahead with every step she took.

She wasn't about to disclose to them that Sébastien had known Josephine du Bois, but she could be honest in her denial. They had never discussed where her great aunt had lived but perhaps he already knew? Her mind was whirling—her foolish innocence was becoming more apparent to her by the minute. In her naiveté she had thought she could cross the ocean, find the necklace, and assume that no one else would be interested in a treasure of emeralds and diamonds.

If indeed Sébastien was looking for the necklace, had she been a fool to trust him? Is that why he had tried to dissuade her? Was the talk of a future in the islands just that—sweet talk to get her to disclose more information about a necklace that he already knew of? Did he laugh when she landed on his boat like a ripe juicy plum for the picking? Mortification filled her as she recalled the nights... and days... she had spent in his bed. She had shed all her girlish modesty.

More than that, it was grief that filled her. Grief for the false love she had believed in. Setting her jaw in determination, Madeleine fought the tears that threatened and summoned the anger to clear her mind. All she could be grateful for was that she hadn't told Sébastien that she loved him. Perhaps it was the premonition of losing him—as she had lost everyone else she had ever loved? Or perhaps a small part of her had told her not to trust.

Lust and love. Had not Aunt Josephine's diary been witness to the same web of lies?

That was something she would have to deal with—if, no, when— she escaped. But perhaps she would not escape, and her life was over?

Would anyone care? She had no one who held concern for her well-being. She was alone, and she would have to help herself. She had crossed the world to find this necklace and by God, she would not give in to three thieves.

"This way." A rough hand shoved her forward and Madeleine lifted her head. They had turned into a quiet street which appeared to be full of grand homes. It was a lot quieter than the other streets. It would be far less likely that someone would notice that she was being held against her will. Most of the houses were in darkness and the street was quiet, apart from a chorus of croaking that came from the far end. As she was dragged down the street, a dog barked, and a light came on.

"It's the last house on the river side before the swamp." Glee filled his rough voice as they approached the last house. It was in darkness and Dirk put his hand up and the two men held her as they stood in the shadows.

"All right, madam. Where will we find the necklace?"

Safe at rest, at home. In the water, by the water, in the garden. Her great aunt's spidery writing was imprinted in her memory like a brand. She would never—even on the threat of death—reveal those words.

"It is…secreted in her…boudoir." Madeline made her voice hesitant as though the words came reluctantly. "There is a wooden chest and it is hidden in a false bottom beneath some garments." She was beginning to warm to her fabrication. "Luxurious silk cloth from the—"

"Enough." Dirk looked around. "We will need the three of us to search the house…and we must be silent. If they are asleep, we may have to—"

Madeleine gasped at the thought that her lie about the whereabouts of the necklace could result in the death of whoever was in the house. "Wait…"

"Be quiet." Dirk came closer and took her arm. 'We cannot afford to have you inside while we search, in case you think to scream and warn them." He looked around and even in the dim moonlight she could see the intention in his eyes as he raised his hands.

"No, please…" Her stomach clenched as his hands circled her neck "What if my aunt has moved it? I know of other places where it may be hidden. You cannot kill me, you may need more information. There is more." She hated begging, but it was her only chance.

His hands stilled, and he let out a snort of disgust, obviously realizing that she spoke the truth. He reached down into his long boot and pulled out a coil of thin rope. "Just as well I had forethought, wasn't it?"

He jerked his head to the vacant land next to the house. Across a low stone fence through the foliage of a large magnolia tree, the tiered vaults in the cemetery shone in the moonlight.

"Tie her to that tree." He moved in until his face was mere inches from hers. "Not a word. Not a sound or a scream from you…or I will come back and slit your throat. I promise you of that."

Chapter Twenty-One

"Captain!" Sébastien recoiled as a small figure bulleted from the darkness and hit him squarely in the stomach. He caught his breath and looked down at a mop of red hair.

"Jake. What in God's name are you doing out at this late hour?" His stomach clenched as the boy began to speak quickly and incoherently. "Slowly. Take a breath and tell me what the matter is."

"They made me. They made me pretend I was saying goodbye." The lad hitched a sob.

"Who did?"

"That scoundrel, Dirk and the other two. They took Miss Madeleine, sir. They took her."

Heat flashed through Sébastien's body and his pulse beat rapidly. He forced himself to calm as he flexed his fingers. Crouching down, he looked the lad in the eye and he spoke firmly. "Just tell me clearly, where did they take her?"

"To the house in Rue Toulouse where the lady with the necklace lives."

"No, lad. That cannot be." Sébastien frowned and shook his head. "That lady is dead and the house is gone."

"Well, that is where they were going when I managed to escape." Jake looked back at him with wide eyes. "They wanted the necklace."

Sébastien's gaze dropped to the lad's neck and realised it was stained with blood. "Did they harm you?"

"It is only a nick. Can I come with you to rescue Miss Madeleine?"

Sébastien stood and looked toward the *Maiden* while he thought. "I need you to help me and it is a very important task that I will give you. I don't have time to write a letter, so you must listen carefully."

Jake nodded and did not speak.

"I want you to go straight to Lafitte's Blacksmith Shop. It is a tavern on the corner of Rue St. Philip."

"I know it, sir."

"That is where you will find my crew. Tell them I need help and I need at least six men. Lead them to the end of Rue Toulouse. Tell them Miss Madeleine is in danger."

The young lad turned away but Sébastien touched his shoulder. "Tell them it is a matter of life and death and to come prepared...and come quickly."

Sébastien took a precious moment to run up the gangplank of the *Maiden*, down to his cabin and threw the berth ticket on the table, not giving any regard to it. He reached above the alcove where Madeleine had first hidden and opened a secret panel at the side. The pistol that he kept secreted there was oiled and ready for use. He tucked it into his boot and ran for the ladder.

***

Madeleine waited only a few minutes after the three men crept around the back of the two-story wooden house. When the man with the strong accent had tied her hands, she had held them apart and it had been too dark for the man to see the gap between her wrists as he had secured the rope. She had even feigned a cry of pain when he had pulled the rope tight and looped it over a branch above her head.

Time was of the essence, and as soon as the men were out of sight, Madeleine slipped her hands from the rope. She gathered her skirts and ran in the other direction as fast as she could without making a sound. If she were to escape them, she must get as far away as she could. As she stepped over the low fence, a shiver ran down her back and the hairs rose on the nape of her neck. Slowly, she walked through the marshy ground to the first row of vaults. It was very different to the church graveyard where her family was buried in the village in England. Long shadows loomed ahead of her as she walked slowly between the two-story vaults. She reached the end of the first row at the back of the cemetery and her feet sank in the soft ground. She lifted her foot and her slipper pulled free with a loud squelch. A slight breeze picked up and a keening sound surrounded her.

It is only the wind blowing around the tombs. But rationalizing the reason for the sound did not stop the goose bumps that rose on her arms.

A dog barked in the distance and as Madeleine turned to the sound, it was followed by a bloodcurdling scream. Lamplight glowed in the upper story of Josephine's old house and guilt ran through her as she feared that the men had killed someone because of her lie about the necklace. Step by step she backed away and stifled a scream as something brushed her hair. Madeleine swivelled around, her hands batting at the air, but it was only a tangle of vines hanging from a tree. The deeper she walked into the cemetery, the thicker the vegetation grew where the swamp had reclaimed the graves.

She looked around as fear crawled up her spine. The only way back to the streets that were filled with light and people, was past the house, and the three men were sure to come out if she went that way. All around her were vaults and crypts leading down to a yawning darkness and she searched for a place away from the side of the cemetery near the house, and high enough to hide behind. The wind picked up and the moon was obscured by a scudding cloud, and the cemetery was plunged into darkness. She closed her eyes as fear crawled in her chest. It was only a short while before the wind dropped and the cloud cleared away. Madeleine opened her eyes and gasped as fingers of mist rose eerily between the vaults. Feeling her way, with her hands outstretched in front of her, she touched a cold slab of marble and walked around to the other side before dropping to the damp ground, her hands over her eyes. Chasing Aunt Josephine's necklace was an impossible dream, she should have realised that happiness and security had been hers to grasp all along—Sébastien wanted to settle down in Hawaii, and if only she had seen that was where true happiness lay—in the future, not in the past.

But now it was too late.

***

All was quiet at the end of Rue Toulouse where Josephine and Francois du Bois had once resided. Sébastien had known the house well, having visited there on a number of occasions to do business with François before he died. The events of this night disturbed him. There was no necklace to be found in the house. The house had been razed to the ground two years ago. He focused on the task at hand, refusing to let thoughts of failure enter his mind. He held onto the hope that Madeleine was still alive. He would not let himself think anything else. A sour taste filled his mouth. She must be safe— he could not fail her, too. Guilt wracked him, and it was like a physical blow to his stomach. He had taken her innocence and now she had been kidnapped because he had left her alone.

He stood beneath the magnolia tree that had once been in Josephine's indoor garden, wondering where they had taken her. As he stared down at the ground deep in thought, the moon shone on a length of rope thrown on to the pavers that had survived the fire. As he bent to pick it up a stealthy movement caught his eye.

"'t is only us, Captain." He recognised the deep voice of his second mate as five more figures materialized in the darkness, followed by the young cabin boy.

"Well done, lad." Sébastien reached down and squeezed his shoulder. "You worked quickly."

"Where is she?" The young boy's voice broke as he struggled to catch his breath.

"I don't know. I am at a loss to understand why she would lead them here."

"Sir," Jake interrupted him. "Miss Madeleine never said to me that the house had burned down. I don't think she knew. She told them it was the last house before the cemetery." He pointed to the next house where a lamp shone softly in the window. "Look."

Sébastien followed Jake's gaze and drew in his breath. A couple of figures were moving stealthily through the room on the top floor of the house and he would wager that one of them was Dirk.

"You're right."

A hushed conversation with the second mate and they devised a plan to surprise the men. Jake was to wait here—in case anyone else came—and Sébastien would look for Madeline in the house while his men overpowered Dirk and his henchmen.

Together they moved to the back of the timber building, their movements masked by the noise of the rising wind. Sébastien looked up, the moon was completely obliterated by cloud and there was a smell of rain in the air.

Chapter Twenty-Two

Madeleine was nowhere to be found. The thieves had been overpowered and restrained and were on the way to the new police building that Carondelet had recently established as a response to the crime in the town. Sébastien's second mate was ministering to the elderly woman who had been alone in the house when the men had broken in. She was crying and shaking her head saying she knew nothing of the chest or a necklace they had insisted was in her room.

Sébastien's despair grew as they searched every room of the house, in case the men had locked Madeleine away. Dirk and the men denied knowledge of her whereabouts, even under the threat of keelhauling. The man with the Creole accent had finally admitted he had tied her up and left her beneath the tree on the vacant lot beside the cemetery.

Sébastien had insisted that Jake go back to town with the crew, but the young cabin boy had refused.

"I won't leave until we find her." Jake was of the same mind as Sébastien. Madeleine was here somewhere; she had to be close by. "Sir, it's not your fault."

Sébastien stood beneath the tree staring over at the cemetery. "Oh, yes, lad. It is. It has been my fault from the minute I chose not to turn back to New Orleans when she was first discovered on the boat." He ran the length of rope between his fingers. "Can we trust that they really have no knowledge of where she is? Or did they kill her when she showed them to the house?" He gave a bitter laugh. "The wrong house. No matter what, I can't wait here. I am going to search here."

"And I." The boy's voice was strong.

"I want you to go to town in case Miss Madeleine has escaped and is wandering around lost. If you find her, take her back to the *Maiden* and get a message back to me."

Jake nodded slowly, obviously seeing the sense in Sébastien's words. He watched as the young lad disappeared into the darkness and then he walked back to the tree. For some unknown reason, he felt closer to Madeleine there. The trunk of the tree was rough on his face as he leaned against it. He closed his eyes as a soft rain began to fall.

I have failed her. If she is dead, I will avenge her death. His dream of the islands no longer held appeal for him and he knew he had made the wrong decision today when he had booked a single birth. He loved Madeleine and she was as necessary to him as the air he breathed. His life would not be worth living if she were gone. He slammed his fist onto the hard bark of the tree in front of him.

What could I have done differently to keep her safe? His chest closed, and he clenched his hands in frustration.

"Sébastien?"

At first he thought he was hallucinating as the soft voice reached him. Opening his eyes, he looked past the tree. Madeleine was walking through the long grass toward him, an ethereal figure coming out of the mist. Her hair was loose and the raindrops on her head glistened in the moonlight. He stumbled back a step, unable to believe his eyes until she held her arms out, wondering if he was seeing a ghost.

"Sébastien?" This time her voice shook and with a deep groan he reached for her and enfolded her in his arms. She was real and warm, and soft against him. He buried his face in her hair and his eyes were wet with tears.

"I thought I had lost you. I thought you were gone from me forever and I could not bear it." His voice was muffled against her thick tresses. "Where did you go?"

"I escaped and hid in the cemetery, but I was so worried that they would hurt someone." Her soft body pressed into his and he tightened his arms around her. He would not let her go.

"I watched from the cemetery while your men took them away. Did they...did they...find the necklace?"

"No." He stepped back and looked at her. "Because you sent them to the wrong house."

Madeleine's shoulders sagged, and she stared at him for a long moment.

"This is where your aunt's house was. We are standing on the pavers that formed her indoor garden. This magnolia tree survived the fire." He put his forehead against hers. "It was a pretty room with tinkling water that came from a fountain that was right here beneath the tree."

As he watched, her eyes widened, and a smile crossed her face.

"Safe at rest, at home. In the water, by the water, in the garden," she whispered. "Now I know."

"What did you say?" He leaned in and framed her face with his hands.

"Nothing. It is no longer of importance. All that matters to me is that you are here…and that you wanted to find me."

He whispered her name and then he brushed her temple with his lips, the relief that she was alive, mingled with the love that he felt for this woman. As his mouth moved to claim hers, he felt the smile that still tilted her lips.

"Of course I did." He would not tell her of his doubts. They were gone and he knew that he would go with this woman to wherever she chose.

Together, they stood for a long time in a close embrace on the pavers.

***

Madeleine had decided that her future lay with Sébastien and not with discovering the family heirloom. She had begun this journey by searching for what she thought would bring her true happiness. If she hadn't started on that path she would not have found Sébastien. He was where she would find her true happiness. She looked down as he held her in his arms. If she was right, the object of her quest was beneath her feet, Great Aunt Josephine had buried it there for a reason and there it would stay. Her diary did not say that it was to be found.

The moon painted a ragged silver edge on the clouds as a chorus of frogs croaked in the cemetery. Sébastien tilted her chin and placed his mouth on hers. His breath mingled with hers as he repeated the question he had asked once before.

"So shall I take you back to England or will you travel with me to the Hawaiian Islands and become my wife?" He stared down at her. "With no regrets?"

"I have no regrets. I will be proud to be your wife and I will come with you to your islands.

Sébastien gathered her close and Madeleine knew she had chosen the right path. She loved her pirate and would follow him to wherever he took her.

"I would follow you to the ends of the earth…without any regrets, my love."

"Shall we investigate further? Seek Josephine's belongings?"

Madeleine shook her head slowly. "No, the necklace can stay safe. I do not believe that it was Aunt Josephine's intention that it be found, but we will never know. Not unless we find her diary."

"Are you sure?"

"I am sure."

Sébastien lowered his head and gently claimed her mouth, and Madeleine smiled just before her lips opened to his. She knew she was loved for herself, and not for any family heirloom.

Epilogue

Madeleine Leclerc sat on the warm sand watching the gentle waves break on the shore. The plump toddler who lay back against her chest sat up and pointed to the water in excitement as a sleek figure swam toward the beach.

"Papa." The little girl squirmed with excitement.

"Yes, Catherine, it is your Papa, and if we are lucky he shall have caught our dinner." Madeleine watched as her husband stood in the clear water and waded toward her.

His black hair was plastered to his head, and his eyes were full of laughter. White teeth flashed in a tanned and ruggedly handsome face and she remembered the first time she had seen his face. But no longer was Sébastien in the muddy waters of the Mississippi River. She looked up at the lush green hills to the house that he had built. Acres of waving sugar cane surrounded the house, and the jeweled sea surrounded their island home. She looked to the east and noticed a boat pulling away from the pier. A red-haired young man ran along the grassy hill toward them.

Sébastien walked from the water and picked up the cloth she passed to him, wiping the water from his face. "Jake appears to be excited about something."

He sat on the sand beside them and Catherine plopped onto her father's lap. "No fish today, my sweet girl."

"Sébastien." Jake waved a parcel as he approached them. "The new seeds have come from Kauai."

"Then we have work to do, Jake." He flicked a lazy grin at Madeleine and the warmth rushed straight to her belly. Even after three years of marriage, he only had to look at her and she turned into the wanton wench he had introduced to the pleasures of love on the *Maiden*.

"Madeleine, there is a letter for you as well." Jake threw a packet into her lap and she picked it up curiously.

She ran her finger along the edge and opened it, pulling out a single piece of paper. "Oh, Sébastien. It is a reply to the letter that I wrote to Uncle Titus last year." She smiled as tears filled her eyes.

"He has travelled back to Bellerose Hall and he has hired back the servants to keep the estate running while he goes on another mission. My drastic action to escape him made him realise how many lives had been changed because of what he had done without thought. He has joined the London Missionary Society and is now in Tahiti. He seems a much softer man, now. And happier."

Happiness overwhelmed her as she read the last few lines of the letter. "He apologises for arranging my marriage and for telling that horrid man about the necklace he had read about in the diary. He tells me that Jed, our gardener, sends his regards and that the roses at Bellerose Hall are more beautiful than ever this year." Madeleine stared across the water. It was thousands of miles to Bellerose Hall. "I only have one regret."

Sébastien held the baby firmly with one hand and took Madeleine's hand with the other. "Do you miss your home so much, my love?"

"No… this is my home." She smiled up at her husband. "I just wonder what became of Aunt Josephine's diary."

"You may never know." Sébastien looked down at Catherine as the baby's little fingers pulled at his wet hair.

Madeleine looked at Sébastien; he was

bronzed and muscled, and his wide smile showed his happiness. She held his gaze steadily and let the love shine from her eyes. "No, we may not. But it does not matter. This is my home, and this is where my heart lies. My happiness is truly complete."

The Emerald Lei
The Heirloom Search: Book 2
by Susanne Bellamy

Eva Abbott sells her inheritance in England, Bellerose Manor, to provide for the care of her nephew. She buys a pineapple plantation in Hawaii but discovers her neighbour, Luc Martineau, will do anything to take it from her.
When Eva discovers a diary which may solve their financial problems, villains follow her to Hawaii and attempt to force her to reveal the whereabouts of the heirloom emerald necklace. Is Luc an ally or an enemy? Is he after Eva or her land?

Sign up to Annie's newsletter so you don't miss out on the release of Books 3 and 4 to complete the series:
http://www.annieseaton.net/

Other books by Annie Seaton

Whitsunday Dawn
Undara

Porter Sisters Series

Kakadu Sunset

Daintree

Diamond Sky

Hidden Valley (2021)

Pentecost Island Series (2020)

Pippa

Eliza

Nell

Tamsin

Evie

Cherry

Odessa

Sienna

Tess

Isla

Bondi Beach Love Series

Beach House

Beach Music

Beach Walk

Beach Dreams

Second Chance Bay Series

Her Outback Playboy

Her Outback Protector

Her Outback Haven

Her Outback Paradise

Love Across Time Series

Come Back to Me

Follow Me

Finding Home (November 2020)

The Threads that Bind (2021)

The Trouble with Paradise

Deadly Secrets

ANNIE SEATON

Adventures in Time

Silver Valley Witch

The Emerald Necklace

Worth the Wait

ABOUT THE AUTHOR

Annie Seaton lives on the edge of the South Pacific Ocean on the east coast of Australia with her own hero of many years. Their two children are now grown up and married, and four beautiful grandchildren have arrived. Now they share their home with Toby, the naughtiest dog in the universe, and Barney, the rag doll puss.

When she is not writing Annie can be found in her garden or walking on the beach...or most likely on her deck overlooking the ocean, camera in hand as the sun sets. Each winter, Annie and her husband leave the beach to roam the remote areas of Australia for story ideas and research. Readers can contact Annie through her website annieseaton.net or find her on Face book, Twitter and Instagram.

Annie loves to hear from readers. annie@annieseaton.net

If you would like to stay up to date with Annie's release, subscribe to her newsletter here: annieseaton.net